MASHED:
The Culinary Delights of Twisted Erotic Horror

An Anthology By

GRIVANTE PRESS

Visit us online at

www.grivantepress.com

Dedicated to all the twisted &
kinky horror lovers out there!

Enjoy this collection
from your like minded brethren.

MASHED is a collection of 17 short stories curated from over 200 submissions, for the purpose of entertaining you with The Culinary Delights of Twisted Erotic Horror.

Inside you will find tales that will excite your curiosity, tingle your taste buds and possibly leave you feeling awkwardly aroused. Dealing with subjects such as ghosts, possessions, demons, biscuits, corn, coffee, cunnilingus and glory holes, these stories might also leave you cringing in horror or crying in laughter. Such is the smorgasbord that is before you.

Consider this a buffet for the senses, but not for those that are faint of heart or easily offended.

-Grivante

Enjoy The Feast!
-JL.

THE MASHED MENU
OF CULINARY DELIGHTS

A WOMAN'S CORN
By J. Donnait

"We can't do this anymore, babe," Lester said.

Tessa paused for a moment, then kept tearing the skin from the cornhusks. She was standing at the counter with her back to Lester, who was sitting at the kitchen table with his legs crossed and his hands casually hugging his knee. Tessa knew how he was sitting—Mr. Cool, one of the many reasons she had fallen hard and fast for him—and couldn't bare seeing him so relaxed. Not after what he had just finished saying. As far as she was concerned, when someone drops a heavy like that before dinner, they should be sobbing and, at the very least, looking you in the eye.

The chair was damp beneath Lester's ass. He looked up and through a hole in the roof. A soft grey light fell into the kitchen, but it didn't do much to brighten the atmosphere. Most of the cupboard doors were missing; half the counter had crumbled with rot and the floor close to the stove was a fat man away from giving in. There was also the distraught woman. She cast her own pall over the room.

"I have to go back home," Lester continued.

She scoffed and shook her head. "I knew it," she spat.

"How did you know?"

"Call it a woman's intuition. I could see it in your body language, the way you've been sitting, slouched and relaxed. It's the posture of a man content with breaking a woman's heart." She rubbed her nose and sniffed. "Or maybe I can read your fucking mind." She turned back toward the cutting board and stood motionless.

Lester got up and walked toward her, certain that each step would send him through the floor and into the depths of hell.

"Don't even bother, Les. Don't you dare try and Band-Aid this by wrapping your skinny little arms around my waist." But she was lying to herself. His arms were firm and chiseled, just like the rest of him. Tessa knew damn well that she wanted nothing else but to be held by him. She wanted to feel him behind her, pulling her into him, his chin rubbing against the side of her head, the bristles of his scruffy beard tickling her cheek. She would spend hours daydreaming about the way he carried himself—the way his hands moved when he talked; his smile; the way that she could tell how funny what she said was from the pitch of his laugh: the higher, the funnier.

There was also something otherworldly about the way he plowed her. Sometimes she thought the foundation of the shack shook with each thrust. She could have sworn that the floorboards in the front hall downstairs had split when he came in her the last time. They had, but obviously he couldn't have caused it, it was clearly bad wood, warped by warm weather, maybe. Lester didn't just hit all the right spots, either; he poked and prodded them perfectly, chasing the moving hot zones inside her, smacking her ass when she thought of it, pulling her hair when she needed it, sending her to climax more times than she could count.

If this was to be their last dinner together—their last time together—she knew it was silly to waste precious time by arguing and saying things you didn't mean. There were better things they could be doing. She had spoken before she thought, though, so to hell with everything if she was going to recant. Tessa was a lot of things, and stubborn was one of them.

Lester traced his two steps back to the chair and resumed his comfortable grip on his knee. He studied her and thought about the curves of her body, which were obscured beneath the silk robe she always wore after sex. He thought she was so sexy in that thing and watching her cook dinner wearing the flimsy sheet pumped blood from his heart to his hard-on. It also made saying goodbye harder because guys thought with two heads—a big one and a small one—and the one between the legs always had a more compelling and logical case.

The knife in her hand knocked rhythmically against the chopping board, slicing up an onion, as he studied her exquisite features. She felt him watching her, then took both hands and pressed them on her backside, running her palms down the length of her rear thighs, wiping her hands on her blouse, giving him a little taste, an *hors-d'oeuvre* before the meal. Her hands went back to the counter and the knife blade and Lester looked at her quizzically as he wondered whether he'd heard the chopping stop while she wiped herself down. He was certain he hadn't, that it had pounded on as he pictured himself pounding her while the headrest of their bed banged against the wall. No matter, he thought. Must have been the droning of hypnosis.

They weren't husband and wife. They weren't even boyfriend and girlfriend. Fuck-buddies was more appropriate, but even that wasn't accurate. Technically, Tessa and Lester had been having an affair for a little over nine months. Both claimed they were married and wore silver bands on their ring fingers. Each talked about their families, how they had met their significant others, and how old their children were. They had these talks in bed when Tessa would nestle her head into his armpit after being fucked six ways from Sunday. It wasn't the most ideal time and place to converse about such things, but it was better than telling each other who they really were and where they were actually from.

They met up a couple of times a week at this abandoned bungalow on the outskirts of Trout Creek, a small town in northern Ontario with a curious history. The house had belonged to Joseph Prine, the priest at the local church, until he disappeared a few years ago. After he vanished, nobody so much as joked about wanting the property, so it fell into disrepair. The electricity still worked on account of the township deciding it would cost more to disconnect the wiring than it would to leave it be.

So there was a hole in the roof. Big deal. And some kids thought it'd be a great idea to smash a couple of windows and tag the side of the house with the word "Fuck" in spray-paint. It didn't matter. The bed was a queen, and the mattress creaked when you sat on it, but the scuffmarks from the headrest riding up the wall were indicators that this baby could still handle its matrimonial duty. Thanks to the genius of some pre-pubescent, pimply punk with a can of paint, Tessa and Lester called their home-away-from-home the Fuck Shack. As far as a place to meet up and get carnal in, it did the trick.

Tessa picked up a large knife from the counter, held it up and turned to Les. He opened his mouth, but she waved the knife back and forth in front of her face. Les understood and pursed his lips sarcastically, like a little girl does when she promises not to tell and seals her lips, runs her thumb and index over them, and closes the invisible zipper, pledging secrecy. He understood that she was upset, most likely angry (if he could judge a person's temperament by how they held a knife, then she was definitely angry right now), but also knew that doing what they were doing —meeting up for sex, cuddles, and a few good laughs— doesn't last forever. If it were supposed to, they wouldn't be holed up in a rundown house on the edge of town.

"I thought we had something good, Les. Maybe it wasn't as real as it should have been and that's a subject we never broached, perhaps for good and perhaps not. The fact that we never spoke about it is tell-all, no? Still. I thought we had something."

Lester nodded and looked down. He thought about how *good* was the measure of a relationship's success these days. Not *great*. Not *amazing*. Just *good*. If it was good, you had hit the big time, so go on and live the good life of constant contemplation, juggling the question, *Am I happy?* He wondered: since when did 'good' become the new 'meh', and by addition, when did mediocrity—in love or lust—become an achievement?

Now that he had seen her face, facing her was a lot harder. Before coming tonight, he had imagined how breaking the news to her would go: they would cry; they would screw (over and over and over again); they would cry while screwing and then leave the house together, sharing one last hug and a final kiss. In his mind, they would part peacefully, their love treaty signed and honored, forever allies who had avoided war. He had prepared himself for an emotional tilt, though, which he knew was a distinct possibility. In either situation, they'd spend the next few days kicking the dirt when walking, their heads hung low and then life would go on.

As if she were reading his mind, she said, "You thought this would be a picture-perfect break-up, huh? It never happens like it does in the movies, Les. The guy always fucks the speech up and the girl always loses her shit. Or vice versa. Either way, it's never amicable and why should it be?" She turned back around and started shaving the corn from the cob with the knife. When she was done, she threw the cobs into the sink and put the corn into a pot. The house smelled like the country, like home—hot salted water and sweet corn mixed with pine.

Tessa bent down and pulled the oven door open, making sure to bend low enough that the entrails of her robe slipped a teensy-weensy bit above her butt cheeks.

Lester let out a half grunt, half moan and then bit his lip.

Tessa grinned a little. She closed the oven door and stood up, fixing the collar of her garment and brushing her hair back over her shoulders. She reached above the stove to where the spice rack was, revealing the small of her ass again, pulled out three containers and placed them on the counter.

Lester fixed his crotch, pulling his jeans to make more room for his little thinker. It took all of his willpower —which was fading and fading fast—to watch Tessa unscrew the lids from the containers and sprinkle salt, pepper and a third spice he couldn't make out into the pot of corn. Tessa stirred the contents, banged the spoon on the edge of the pot and then chopped a carrot with the force and grace of someone beating a six-inch nail into a piece of knotted oak.

She whispered into the pot as she poured the chopped onions and carrots and emptied the saucer of cream in it.

"Why are you talking to the food?" Lester asked.

"It, uh, sweetens the pot." She stared to sob. "Grub tastes better when it feels loved."

Lester fidgeted in his seat, stretched his neck from

side to side. "Is it the onions?" He wasn't the best with uncomfortable situations.

If Tessa heard him, she didn't act like it. She leaned further into the pot, the steam turning her skin to a waxy film. A wad of snot drooped slowly from her nostril until it plopped into the pot and sizzled along with the other vegetables. Lester winced.

Tessa straightened up and rubbed her nose. She turned to Lester. Her collar had magically loosened, exposing the tits that fit perfectly into Lester's palm to the open air. Lester smiled, even though he felt like he could feel himself frowning below the belt.

Tessa followed Lester's stare to her chest, shrugged and then looked back up. She didn't bother fixing herself. She didn't really want to. She was willing to bet that Lester was doing a lot of thinking with both of his brains and it was causing him agony. You always wanted what you shouldn't have.

"Where's 'home', Les?"

Lester's smile faded. "It doesn't matter. Far from here, and that's about all I want to say on it."

Tessa frowned and pulled her robe closed. "You can do better than that, hun."

He shifted his ass so that he was sitting up straight, uncrossed his legs, and placed his hands on his thighs. People always have a tic when they lie and this was Lester's. "Toronto, Tess. Close enough to here that it hurts to have to end it, but far enough that it can't keep on."

Tessa watched him indifferently with her blank stare.

She raised her eyebrow and tilted her head. It was her are-you-fucking-kidding-me face. *Surely he can do better than that.* She pictured him in a Keep Calm And Carry On To Toronto t-shirt, except instead of a crown separating the words in the middle it was a picture of his smiling face.

"That's the biggest pile of shit to come out of your mouth tonight and you've been spraying dung all evening." She turned back to the stove and stirred the pot again.

A few hundred yards away, two kids stopped at the end of the street that led to the Fuck Shack. They were going to go and knock out a couple more windows, but thought the better of it. Tonight didn't feel right. Kids don't often follow their gut, but there was a delicious scent of home cooking in the air, so tonight their tummies were screaming and they paid attention. They kicked off and continued over the train tracks and back home to their cozy and warm dining rooms, toward images of roast beef, creamed corn, and chocolate chip cookies and milk.

Lester stood up and stretched, his fingertips nearly touching the ceiling. "What does it matter, Tess?" He walked past Tessa, whose hands were planted on the edge of the stove as the handle of the wooden spoon spun in the pot, lifting the contents and turning them over with a blink. He paused, blinked, and shook his head, wiggling his cheeks. The spoon was erect and stationary in the pot. He shrugged and continued through the doorframe and toward the front door. He didn't dare try and kiss her goodbye, even though he wanted to drill the living shit out of her. Did she have to cook looking so damn sexy? When he got to the door, he turned toward the kitchen. The hallway wall obscured half of Tessa, so he could still see enough of her that he could technically say he left while looking at her. Lester opened his mouth.

Tessa thought, *He better not say it. He better not say some corny, cliché bullshit.*

"It was fun while it lasted, Tess," he said and opened the door.

Tessa dropped the spoon from her hand and whipped her right arm like she was slapping an invisible child. The doorknob tore from Lester's hand and the door slammed shut on his face. He expected as much considering her initial reaction to the news, but he figured he would have been on the outside looking in, not the other way around.

Lester backed away from the front door until he was standing beside Tessa, not looking at her. His eyes were still fixed on the door that he didn't shut and that Tessa was ten feet away from. "What in the world was that, Tess? Did you see that? The fucking door closed by itself. Think it was the wind?"

Tessa horked and spat into the pot. "Yeah, that's what it was, alright. Go and sit down. Supper's almost ready."

He turned his head, looked at her, then the pot and back at her. He could see a wad of chunky, green spit bubbling on top of the yellow of the corn. He wrinkled his nose in disgust and backed away from her, further into the kitchen. "That's the second secret ingredient you've put in there. I'm losing my appetite. And why are you making a pot of cooked corn? Who the hell eats that? You didn't even put butter in it! And what have you got in the oven? Please tell me it's shepherd's pie or a sixty pound turkey. Something you haven't drooled onto."

"Nope. Nothing in the oven," she said. She took a big whiff of the pot and then turned and faced Lester, her hands held behind her back like an innocent little schoolgirl. All that was missing were the pigtails.

"Then why did you open it and check inside?" he asked.

"Because I wanted to make your decision tougher on you. I wanted you to see my hot bod. I wanted you to think about it all the way *home*. Judging by how often you were playing with your jeans, pulling and shifting and pulling and shifting, I'd say that your mind was awful busy. Busier than your hands, even. Either that or you're learning to drive stick and you were practicing with your shaft." She smiled the smile of verbal checkmate.

Lester scoffed. "You're unbelievable. I hope your next gent is a limp-dick who's allergic to Viagra. I have to go. See-yuh!"

Before he could take a step forward, Tessa flashed her hands from behind her back and made a shoving motion toward Lester. He flew back and hit the seat with his ass hard enough that the floorboards cried as the legs of the chair slid backward by a foot. She then pointed at his wrists and his ankles, shooting at them with her index finger like a kid with an imaginary gun.

Lester sat stunned for a second and then tried to lunge out of the chair. He nearly ate the floor, because when he tried to get up, he found he was bound to the chair by… nothing? He felt a cold and tight pressure on his wrists and ankles. When he tried to lift his arms, his wrists stuck to the arm of the chair. When he tried to kick out his legs, his ankles wouldn't budge.

"What the fuck, Tess? What's happening?"

She shrugged and then grinned. "Scared, Lester? A lot of things happening by something or someone you can't see. Must be unsettling. Let me ask you a question."

Lester assumed that Tess was going to ask him who he really was, which was something he didn't want to divulge, but he was more concerned with what was happening to him.

"How hard are you now, darling?" she asked.

Lester didn't seem to hear the sexual jab. He was too busy looking wildly around the kitchen for whatever it was that had shut the door on him and pinned him where he sat. He tried wrenching himself out of the chair again, bucking to and fro, side to side and hopping up and down. The legs of the chair pecked at the floor, *clack-clack*, but he couldn't free himself from whatever was holding him prisoner. He was panting and over the sharp inhales and exhales, he could hear Tessa chuckling.

He stopped fighting the chair and looked at Tessa. Out of breath, he asked, "You're… doing… this?"

She gasped and started clapping. "Look at you! You've figured it out. Would you like your prize now or later?"

He tried lifting his wrists again—not as rough this time—and let out a defeated moan. "But h… How?"

"My sweetheart; my hunny-bunch. You might have thought I've been acting like a bitch since you decided to shred my heart and you're a little right. You'd be closer to the truth if you removed one of the letters from 'bitch' and replaced it with another. Can you figure it out, darling? Or should I spell it out for you?" She turned to the pot and took another big whiff.

"I don't want to play anymore fucking games, Tess. Let me go!" He was starting to huff and puff again, not from the cardio of trying to free himself, but from the anger that boiled inside him. He could feel it burn in his chest. One room, two hearts on fire.

She looked over her shoulder at him. "Aww, be-be," she said, pouting, "You're no fun. Allow me to help you." She turned around and faced him. "I'm a witch. See? That wasn't so hard. I couldn't be a hitch, pitch or ditch, and those were your only other choices. You had a twenty-five percent chance of being right if you took a shot in the dark; but, if you thought hard for a fraction of a second, you would have come up with the right answer. Now, are you hungry? I'm *famished*."

Lester scrunched his eyebrows and flinched. "A witch? What the hell are you talking about?"

Tessa rolled her eyes. "You know, *Wizard of Oz*, Salem, broomsticks and potions, hexes and burning at the stake? Though most of that stuff is romanticized, you seem to need help with understanding things tonight, so I'm trying to dumb it down for you. Got it now, kiddo?"

Lester did. A part of him reasoned that it had been clear all along. She had a supernatural prowess in bed, defying the odds of physiology with her flexibility and stamina. And making him cum like nobody had before. Let's not forget that. He did fall in love with her after their first fuck and meal, which was pretty fast—almost too fast for Cupid to draw back his bow. She did cook that night, too. Could there have been a potion involved? It had to be magic. Or coincidence. Michael Jordan wasn't a wizard (owner of that team eventually, sure), but he played with other-worldly abilities. Tessa was just really good at sex, born with the gift of coitus. Her mother had taught her how to cook, without the use of a cauldron or a wren's liver or ocelot's spleen. Maybe mother informed her about the spell sex could cast on a man and suggested—possibly even showed her—how to be good enough to entrance and control.

Tessa watched him closely. "Thinking, are we? Pray tell."

Lester snapped out of his stupor and chuckled. He had loved her—really and truly—and his reason for leaving her had nothing to do with his supposed kids and wife. Distance was the only safe thing for Tessa and Lester had tried to give her that. Tonight was full of revelation and so now it was Lester's turn to start telling the truth.

"If you're a witch, then I'm the fucking devil," he said.

Tessa frowned and snapped her fingers. Lester's lips slammed closed like the front door had on his face. He tried to open his mouth, but supernatural superglue kept his lips stuck. "I've had enough of your negativity, Les. I'd like some silence before we eat." She returned to her pot. She bent over it, her face nearly inside, and whispered things that Lester couldn't make out. Tessa had to shush him a couple of times when he was humming too much, trying to talk through his sealed mouth.

After a minute, she removed her face from the pot and snapped her fingers once. Lester's jaw dropped and hung open as if a cinder block were hanging from his chin. Tessa took a ladle and scooped out a single heap of corn and plopped it into a bowl. She took a soup spoon from the drawer, picked up the bowl and walked to the kitchen table. She sat down beside Lester and turned her chair away from the table to face him. She hooked her feet to the feet of his chair and pulled it toward her until their knees were almost touching. All Lester needed was a bib and the plastic table that accompanied a baby chair and you had the perfect photo op for a really fucked up re-creation of a mother feeding her child.

Tessa rested the bowl in her lap, stirred the corn around and brought the spoon up and held it between their faces. Single kernels slopped from the pile of corn and onto Tessa's lap and the floor.

Lester focused on the spoon which crossed his eyes. Tessa looked past the spoon, saw Lester's cockeyes and laughed.

"Aww," she said, still laughing, "You look so *cute*! Now, open wide—as if you have a choice—and let the aero-plane land." She hummed and rippled her lips, which started the engines of the spoon. She flew it toward his mouth, hitting turbulence and air pockets here and there, swooshing and swirling it up and down, side to side.

Lester recoiled and tried to tell her to stop, but ended up sounding like a deaf person trying to argue. His jaw was weighed down too far so that his tongue couldn't formulate a word.

The spoon-plane made its landing in the hangar of Lester's mouth. He moved his tongue around and stuck it out, fighting to push the warm and salty corn from the back of his throat.

Tessa stood up, grabbed a handful of hair on the back of Lester's head and pulled. His head snapped back so that his mouth was parallel with the ceiling. He whipped his tongue in and out, spilling a couple of kernels from the corner of his mouth, still trying to keep the corn from forcing its way into his stomach.

Tessa grinned as she thought about how many times she'd seen his tongue move like that when it was buried between her legs. She was past regret, had left heartbreak far behind. She was too mad to believe that she had ever loved him.

She used her free hand to snap her fingers, shutting his mouth once more. She plugged his nose and waited for twenty seconds until she saw his Adam's apple jiggle up and down and then, as if it were sighing, lift and fall with a long, deep and desperate gulp. She let go of his head and snapped her fingers a final time, freeing him from the spell.

Lester felt the weight lift from all over his body. There was no longer any pressure on his wrists or ankles and he finally had control of his mouth. He gasped in all the air he could and then doubled over with his hands just above the knee and started coughing.

Then he felt dinner kick in.

It started in the pit of his stomach as if a bouquet of poison ivy bloomed there. He felt it scratch and burn through his bloodstream, branching out to the rest of his body.

Tessa backed away from him and stood in the centre of the kitchen, just under the hanging light. It created a kind of halo above her head and Lester thought—despite death coursing through his veins—that she looked like an angel.

"How does it taste, Les? It's a recipe that my mother taught me and my grandmother taught her and so on. The spit is the secret ingredient to the, well, it's kind of like a poison. I've cooked a few in this very kitchen. The old priest that used to live here is dead, all right. He was a sacrifice a few years ago and a very filling one at that. It's not every day you can get a man of God to break his sacred vows in order to break a woman in; but, when you do? You're set for a while."

She started tearing and her voice became shaky. "You weren't supposed to be a sacrifice. You also weren't supposed to break my heart." Now the sprinklers in her eyes turned on full-blast. "But you did! I thought we had something, Les! More than something! It was all just bullshit! And rather than let you walk out, I decided that I wanted to watch you die. I figured that I may as well get something out of this, too. And I did. I'll look younger. I'll look sexier. And it's all thanks to you and the dinner that's turning your blood to lead. Hell hath no fury like a woman's corn." She laughed and then snorted the snot that was just touching her upper-lip back into her nose.

Lester, still doubled over, craned his head to look at her. His face had turned maroon and the veins in his neck and forehead looked like green worms trapped under his skin.

As if the scared look in his eyes were begging the question, *Why?* she said, "A witch has to take a human being every once in a while and offer it to the Dark Lord."

Lester grunted and struggled to sit up. When his back touched the back of the chair, he croaked, "Which would be me, Tess."

Tessa tilted her head and said, "Wuh?"

Lester cleared his throat and said again, this time more clearly, "Which would be me, Tess."

He groaned like a weightlifter does when they're bench-pressing their max. It got louder and filled more of the room. Soon it was inside Tessa's head and she slapped her cupped hands over her ears. His voice dropped two octaves, turning the groan into the rumble of an earthquake. The dishes and cutlery started to rattle and jingle. The hanging light at the centre of the room, which only moments before hung heaven-sent over Tessa's head, bobbed up and down like a Yo-Yo. The pot on the stove hopped on the burner and then fell, spilling corn across the floor, which seemed to dissolve into a broth until it smoked and hissed as it disappeared through the flimsy wooden planks.

Tessa watched, her face wrinkled with worry and fear, as Lester unhinged his jaw, creating a hole three times the size of a normal open mouth. He gagged, each convulsion stronger and more violent than the last. He slid his tongue out, flat, like when the doctor told you to say *ah*. It reached his chin. Tessa held her breath as it slid even lower, stopping just below his throat. She wondered, for a second, why he had never done that while he was going down on her.

A piece of corn floated from his mouth and hovered in the air a foot in front of his face. A second piece came out, then another and another, until there was a spoonful's worth suspended in midair.

He twirled his hands around the cloud of corn, the right hand on top and turning counterclockwise, the left hand underneath and clockwise. The food spun and moved closer together until it formed a ball the size of a walnut. He stopped spinning his hands and started kneading the food—without actually touching it—like a pitcher rubs a baseball in his palms to warm the leather for better grip.

Tessa was mesmerized by the magic of it all. Her eyes and head rotated with each twirl of the food-ball. Her mouth opened a little when she saw how tight the food had been packed while he was somehow pressing it together without touching it.

Lester stopped phantom-massaging the ball. He held out his right hand, palm up and watched as the ball rose and hovered over it. Tessa, still fascinated, managed to break from her hypnosis and looked at Lester. He met her gaze and then smiled that beautiful smile she loved. His smile made her forgive. It made her want to undo everything that had happened and everything she had done. Her cheeks started to rise, but before she could smile back, Lester grabbed the ball and whipped it at her face. It struck her in the left eye with the force of a bullet. She felt it hit the bone under the eyebrow—heard the crack of it shattering—and felt the socket implode. Hundreds of slivers of agony caught fire behind her eye. It spread further back until the whole left side of her head was ablaze with torturous heat.

She screamed and fell backward, clutching her eye. She landed on a patch where the wood was no good. When she hit the floor, the rotten boards gave way with a wet and hollow *thunk*. She sunk through with ease, like a large rock tossed into a lake covered with a thin sheet of ice. She landed ass-first on the crawlspace floor, three feet down.

Lester sauntered toward the hole, leaned over on his tippy-toes and looked down at Tessa. She was ass to the ground, coughing and sobbing, both blood-soaked hands covering her eye.

"Your mother should know that she can't cook worth shit. That was one terrible recipe. Now it's your turn to take a seat, Tess," he said with boyish glee.

She twitched when he spoke. She had forgotten he was there and suddenly remembered through the shock of it all that he was the reason she was half blind and three feet below the kitchen. She looked up at him with her one good eye. "What *are* you?"

He said, "I'm the Devil, my love." The amusement had left his voice. It was cold and almost indifferent, the tone of a guy down on his luck but willing to see what could happen. Tessa had never heard him talk like that before.

She had never truly been scared before, either—being a witch came with some pretty cool perks—but she was trembling now. Her voice quivered when she spoke. "What are you going to do me?"

"I'm going to consume you," he answered matter-of-factly.

Her lips trembled, which stoked the pain in her head and brought it to an inferno-level throb. "B-b... But if I make sacrifices to you, my liege, and we both grow stronger, why would you—"

"—Kill you?" He barked a single laugh, *Hah!* and then puckered his lips in an unimpressed duck-face. "I thought you were the smart one, Tessa. You gave me shit for not figuring your little ruse out—and by the way, I was one step ahead of you the whole way, but I wanted to make sure you got to have some fun, too—yet now you can't seem to add one and one together. How *very* disappointing."

She thought about telling him not to call her *Tessa*, that he never called her that before, but she couldn't. This man was never really Lester. Lester was an act, a trap.

He continued. "Because I, too, need to feast every once in a while and your power is tremendous. Having a normal mortal is like eating fast food dinner—you feel full before bed, but when it's time to sleep, your stomach starts to rumble. When you wake up in the morning, your tummy feels like a cave." He patted his belly to prove the point. "You, though, are a healthy, balanced meal full of vital proteins and nutrients."

"You're a liar!" she whined. "You wanted to leave. You wanted to spare me."

He laughed. Her intuitive ability was always uncanny. "And not break your heart? Not have you hate me and love me at the same time? I feed on your body, but I live off of your soul. Emotions are powerful and the more there are—the more conflicted they are—the tastier."

"Please," she begged. "Just let me go. You loved me, Les. Love me now." She took her hands from her face, revealing the hole where her eye used to be. Lester laughed. There were pieces of corn stuck to the blood in and around her socket. It was funny the same way watching a skier hit a tree was funny: you didn't expect it and you couldn't help see the comedy first before the shock took over. Sucks to be you, glad it ain't me.

Tessa turned onto her knees and started crawling away.

He stepped forward. "You thought you were going

to sacrifice me? Sweetheart, you're the lamb now. And after all of the waiting I had to do for a spoonful of fucking corn, I am quite peck-ish. So, if you don't mind." He jumped down the hole, feet first and landed on all fours like a jackal. Tessa tried to scream, but the tears and snot running down her throat choked it.

Lester pounced on her. His neck snapped back, the trapdoor in his throat exposing canines the size of hanging icicles, saliva and blood dripping from the yellow stalactite teeth. He laughed; he growled; he filled the world with the screams of children and the cries of grown men begging for mercy. And then he devoured her, body and soul.

The meal didn't sit well with him, which meant that he couldn't have any dessert, which meant that he would continue to feel down and out for the rest of the evening, at least. Tessa turned and turned in his stomach until she exited through the rear the next afternoon. He felt better then, but his mind was still back at the Fuck Shack as he drove up Highway 11 toward Destination Unknown. Those were good times and Tess was a good girl. One of the best. Maybe the next meal would brighten his spirits. He'd make fast food of this one, this time, regardless of sexual prowess or supernatural affiliation. Lesson learned.

-END

To learn more about the author, J. Donnait,
find his author bio at http://www.grivantepress.com/

CHARLIE'S CHUNKY MUNCHING MEAT
By Stephen McQuiggan

Murder.

Charlie rolled the word around his mouth like a hot chip but could not bring himself to utter it. He looked around the drab confines of his cell and tried to take it all in, but he would have a lifetime to do that and there really wasn't that much to see. He prayed for his sister's visit, checking his watch constantly, but time crawled by more slowly now he was aware of it. Charlie had lots of time; he had been sentenced to life imprisonment for murder and all because of a CHUM™ sandwich.

When some men take alcohol they turn into wife-beaters. When some men take drugs they turn into thieves. When Charlie Walls took a CHUM™ sandwich, he turned into a pair of panties; one slice of the sickly pink meat was sufficient to transform him into the nearest female's undergarments and in that form he would stay until she deigned to remove them.

It hadn't always been this way. He could remember childhood picnics, fighting off ants and aunts from the sandwiches, wolfing CHUM™ down with youthful gluttonous abandon. Nothing inappropriate ever occurred; he remained the chubby little boy he had always been. There had been countless weddings of poor relations where CHUM™ was compulsory fare and he had scoffed it throughout the reception between rivers of cheap German beer and nothing untoward had happened to make the bride blush further.

But one day as he sat working late in the office, swamped by the accounts of wealthier and happier men, he nibbled errantly at a CHUM™ and lettuce on rye and found himself wrapped inexplicably around the thighs of big Donna, the office slut.

Donna, like most fat people Charlie knew, was a stranger to the concept of hygiene and it was over a week later before Charlie found himself lying in her laundry basket in a skid-marked shirt; he climbed unseen from her bathroom window, putting his misadventure down to sleepwalking. For the next few days, he suffered from vivid uncanny nightmares where he tottered perilously on the edge of a vast hair strewn canyon.

He explained away his absence from work by feigning illness and his colleagues were quick to comment on how pale and drawn he still looked; when Donna arrived in late, hitching at her skirt and announcing that her panties were simply eating her, they wondered perhaps if they should call a doctor for him.

He took some time off instead, visiting his mother to placate her habitual animosity toward his bachelor status and to save his phone from melting from all the visceral pleas she poured down it like boiling oil every other night.

She asked politely, as is a mother's way, of his job (*are*) and his flat (*you*) and his plants (*seeing*) and his friends (*anyone*) and was he eating enough? He looked rather thin; didn't he know Primrose oil would clear up that spot malarkey on his nose in a trice? A million inane, inept questions that were the vanguard for the great assault (*When are you going to get married and give me grandchildren you selfish little bastard?*) that was always left unsaid.

Charlie didn't mind the head games, all in all, he was genuinely pleased to see the old girl; it was nice to be made a fuss of and she was still the best damn cook a man could wish for. A few years away from home, living on a steady diet of microwave noodles and boil in the bag curries had left him with the physical attributes usually reserved for people on Famine Relief posters.

A dream of roast potatoes had lured him here, of chicken and sprouts and mum's homemade gravy and perhaps a sherry trifle for afters, but with one wayward slip of the tongue, he lost all hope of those culinary delights.

When asked what his immediate plans were he had replied without thinking, "Oh, the usual, pissing the weekend up the wall." He noticed his mother's stern set of jaw too late to turn back; mother didn't like smutty words and 'pissing' was smutty bordering on filthy in her well-thumbed book.

She stormed off into the kitchen to whip up two rounds of CHUM™ and tomato (a double act in the same vein as Hitler and Himmler) and brought them to him with a look that said, "If I wasn't worried about breaking one of my good plates I'd thump you up the snot-box with this."

She went back into the kitchen to wash up some of the crockery she seemed to keep perpetually dirty in anticipation of family upheaval; he could hear her clanking the plates together, spelling out 'Piss indeed' in Morse code and sighing to herself in the confines of her martyrdom. Charlie ate the sandwiches as quickly as he could. The last thing he needed was the 'people starving in Africa' lecture which would surely get an airing at the waste of so much as a crumb.

But before he had time to chew his crusts, he found himself wrapped around the loins of his origin. He felt his mother pluck him hastily from between her smutty place and issue a little sigh. It was a dreadful experience and one that left Charlie frantically trying to recall if his mother ever had that bowel operation, the one she said would tighten her stool. Even if the smell was familiar and strangely comforting, he could not wait to be free; it was one thing to be close to your mother but....

He came to in her muddy back garden with two clothes pegs still attached to his shoulders, surrounded by certain female apparel he would grow ever more used to. His mother found him and thought his threat of drunken debauchery issued the previous day had been carried out;

she'd noticed how quickly he had disappeared when she went to the kitchen, just like his no-good drunk of a father. She hadn't even had time to tell him about the lovely clean little girl who had just moved in next door and how single she appeared to be.

He fled before she could vent the full force of her Christian spleen upon him. He had more than a few things to think about, but a life of tea totalitarianism was definitely not one of them. As obnoxious as spending an entire day girded around his mother's festering love hole had been, he simply could not put it down to sleepwalking, or a hallucination brought on by overwork, as he had done with fat Donna's putrid pot.

No, this had been real; he looked for connections and it didn't take him long to put two and two together and come up with CHUM™. Over the next few days he experimented with a feverish intensity he had never felt before; as with all great endeavors though, his first efforts at Kafkaesque transformation were abject failures.

First, there was Tracey from the upstairs flat. One night as he watched her leave, instead of hiding behind the curtains and rubbing his crotch, he followed her. At an appropriate moment, he slipped out a tin of CHUM™ and, thinking 'I'm Popeye the Pervert man', guzzled down the rancid poor man's steak until he was miraculously nuzzled against his neighbor's voluminous arse.

It was heaven. For half an hour.

Some greasy tool monkey from the local garage gave her a lift and in no time at all Charlie ended up in her handbag. He exploded from the faux leather in a storm of sanitary towels and lipsticks, causing Tracey to bounce off her lover's lap and crack her head on the sunroof. He ran from the car into the cover of some nearby trees, trying to convince himself that although he had frightened them both into premature cigarettes, he had not been recognized.

Then came Sara who worked in accounts and whose thighs were the talk of the toilets. He snuck behind her in the stationery cupboard and one mouthful later got to see just how she kept those thighs so firm. He spent the rest of the morning being slowly suffocated by lycra as Sara indulged her passion for exercise bikes, rowing machines and countless other forms of unnatural madness down at the local gym. It took her a good ten minutes using her long cruel fingernails to pry him out of her sweat sodden bangle before discarding him under her bed.

He was off work for a fortnight after that, he simply couldn't move; but though his back seemed to be broken, his spirit remained intact.

He discovered Malandra on the bus home one evening; she was the kind of perfection he had only previously seen in adverts for tooth-rotting substances. He followed her for the remainder of the week, convinced that he had finally found his special one. She lived in a lovely little suburb ten miles from the city centre, catching the bus every day to the shop where she worked; *Lingering Lingerie* —a store that catered to every red-blooded male's (or pink blooded transvestite's) taste in the feminine undergarment, be it lace, satin, rubber or shaving foam.

Charlie hung around the shop watching her avidly; peeking out from behind the peek-a-boo bras, sweating frantically behind the leather cat-suits. It was all too good to be true. Not only would he become the panties of a sex siren, he would also be the hottest pair of panties imaginable.

After a week of trailing her to make sure she had no bad habits (such as excessive exercise or mood swings brought on by heavy menstruation) Charlie, his eyesight impaired from recent strenuous bouts of violent masturbation, made his move.

It would be nice to think Charlie got his wish, that he spent the rest of his life adorning Malandra's creamy hips, caressing her peachy buttocks, surrounding her holiest of holies and guzzling CHUM™ in between to remain there.

Yes, it would be nice to think he made it and lived happily ever after in his golden snatched cottage, but he didn't.

Life's like that.

Live with it.

After two blissful days on his vulva vacation, Charlie's world came crashing down; Malandra's Greek boyfriend returned from visiting his relatives in a Soho strip joint and spent his first day back attempting to rewrite the Kama Sutra.

At first, this didn't bother Charlie; it was obvious that a girl like Malandra would have a plague of admirers. In fact, during his surveillance, he had seen a long procession of vermin accompany her home and rattle her headboard long into the night. He didn't mind she was a pied-piper, if truth be told, it rather excited him; there was sure to be a surplus of bodily fluids to bubble Jacuzzi-like around him when she slipped him back on. If he had wanted a virgin, he would have sneaked into a convent with a hamper full of his precious pink meat.

But what Charlie hadn't counted on was the sexual degradation peculiar to Manos, Malandra's Mediterranean lover. On the night that was to change his life forever, Charlie lay draped invitingly over his beloved's pudenda, bathing in her juices. Manos, his jeans jutting out alarmingly, leapt on top of her and tried to swallow her face as Charlie felt himself dampen and prayed that the lusty Greek would probe his fingers through him before he was removed.

"Oh Malandra!" moaned Manos. "You're so sexy, I'm gonna eat those panties right offa you!"

There was a scream, an explosion, a muffled "Oh sheeeet!" as Charlie, reborn inside the body of the doomed horn-dog, erupted through the unfortunate Greek's ribcage, sending Manos' skull shooting to the ceiling like a child's rocket. The police found Charlie curled fetal-like on the floor, a foreigner's innards wrapped like jewelry around his sodden, trembling body.

"CHUM™," he told them; "Porridge," they replied.

Murder.

He still couldn't bear to think about that word but he had a long time to practice. A lifetime.

Where the hell was his sister? She was late, and the guards were strict about visiting times. He needed to see her, needed someone to say they understood and loved him no matter what, someone to cry for him.

And there she was, Eileen, sweet Eileen.

She sat behind the shatterproof glass with her quivering lips and her Bambi eyes; she raised her hand and pressed it up against the glass the way she'd seen them do in all the prison movies.

"Oh, Charles," she said, as the tears flowed.

"Oh Eileeth," slurred Charlie, his mouth full of CHUM™ he had smuggled from the canteen in his boiler suit.

What the hell, he thought; Eileen always had a cute ass.

-END

To learn more about the author, Stephen McQuiggan,
find his author bio at http://www.grivantepress.com/

HALLOWEEN NOSH
By Brandon Ketchum

A still-beating human heart twitched in a pool of gore on a cutting board on the dining room table. Wiping sleep from my eyes, I slid into a chair. I rolled up my bathrobe sleeve, curled my fingers around the thumping organ and picked it up. Lifeblood squirted from severed valves onto my wrist and forearm. A single tear squeezed from the corner of my eye.

"She gets me," I murmured, smiling to myself. "She really gets me."

I thumbed the red tear from my eye and set the heart down. A good distraction from my traditional Halloween depression.

"Happy Valentine's Day, my smoofy Vlassy bear," a honeyed voice called to me from the kitchen.

Illyana leaned against the door frame, a martini glass brimming with blood held in each hand. A crimson nightgown hung open over a frilly red bra and panty set, contrasting the smooth pale skin beneath. She sashayed over, placed a glass before me and wiped the blood from my arm with a napkin.

"I appreciate the outfit, and the nosh and bevy, Illy dear, but it's not Valentine's Day. It's... a different holiday tonight."

"It's not Halloween anymore. I decided to shake things up a bit."

Blood rushed to my head at the mere mention of the word. "Halloween! Every year thousands of stupid little ankle-biters dress up in those ridiculous namby-pamby lace and cape getups like my decrepit second cousin, and traipse around begging for candy." I banged a fist into the palm of my hand. "And those pitiful excuses for tricks! Egging houses, toilet paper in trees. Why, back in the old country, we'd get up to real tricks. Entrails in your pillow case, human buffets, wolves in —"

She booped my nose with a finger and made a cartoony sound effect to go with it. "Come on, Vlasta. You're starting to sound like a grumpy old Nosferatu. Drink up."

"Sorry, Illyana." I picked up my glass. "Noroc."

"Noroc," she echoed, then tipped her glass against mine.

We drank.

"Mmm." I ran a finger around the rim of the empty glass and sucked it clean. "How exquisite, Illy. It's rich, without being overly clotted. How did you manage?"

"It's all in the subject, dear. He was young, and ate lots of red meat, which means high cholesterol, and—"

"—fatty tissue. This heart's going to be so tender."

"I'll fetch some crackers," she said.

I stared at her ass as she padded into the kitchen. "I'll carve."

Later, I washed down a bite with a sip of blood. "Tell me again about this Valentine's in October thing, Illy."

She nibbled the edge of a cracker and a chunk of heart, then dabbed at her lips with a napkin. "It's quite simple, darling. Halloween's been a sore spot with you for centuries, but I know how much you used to love it. Stalking prey, blood rites, our annual witching hour cemetery rendezvous... it was the best night of the year. Then Vlad came along and ruined everything for us.

"Well, I'd like to recapture that magic. I've decided we're going to celebrate Valentine's on Halloween, and Halloween in February. Time for us to have our humans and eat them too."

"Just like that?"

Illyana's eyes smoldered as she met my gaze. "Just like that."

I grasped her hand atop the table and gave a wolfish grin. "Why not? We can terrorize the world in February, Illy. I assume you have a wild and romantic All Hallows' Eve planned tonight?"

"You bet." She led me by the hand from the dining room, toward the stairs.

"I like where this is going," I said, eyes drifting to her ass again.

"Naughty, naughty. I may have to punish you for that later."

"Promises, promises." We passed the stairs and went to the basement door. "Speaking of, are we going to the dungeon? I'd say that's promising."

"Go on, see what's lurking below."

I was so excited I took the stairs two at a time. The dungeon, all supple leather and dark tile rather than rusted metal and crusty stone, had a giant padded bondage bed as a centerpiece. Stretched spread-eagle atop it lay a delectable young redhead, her body hidden beneath a white sheet. She blubbered against a black ball gag, drool seeping out over her lips. The human's head thrashed from side to side as we loomed over her.

Illyana stretched on the table alongside her, and I curled up on the human's other side. Her eyes pleaded for release.

"What a wonderful surprise," I said to my mate.

She reached under the sheet and languorously stroked a finger up and down. The human shuddered and leaned away from her, snuggling against me in the process. My body warmed in response, and I became instantly aroused.

"Do you know where I got the drinks and hors d'oeuvres we just enjoyed upstairs?"

"The heart and blood? There's no telling."

"Guess." Her tone teased me, stroking my ears as she continued stroking the girl. This caused the human to grind her hip harder into me as she sought escape from Illyana, inflaming me further.

"I, I don't know," I gasped.

Illyana locked eyes with the human, and she grinned. "Her husband, of course."

The human screamed while I laughed. Illyana slapped her across the face. "Food doesn't scream." This reduced the human to pitiful mewling sounds.

"You're such a romantic."

"It's all for you, Vlassy bear."

"I love you, Illy pooh." I whipped the sheet away and leaned over the human's neck. "You first."

"After you, darling, I insist."

I smiled at her. "Together, then."

She smiled back, showing off her pearly fangs. "Together."

We threw our legs over the human and our arms over each other, and proceeded with our Halloween—or, rather, our Valentine's Day—feast.

-END

To learn more about the author, Brandon Ketchum, find his author bio at http://www.grivantepress.com/

BISCUIT: A LOVE STORY
By Grivante

I. Market Day

Golden beams washed away the night's chill as the sun rose on the horizon. A group of bluebirds perched in the old oak at the edge of the park let loose their morning song. Chirping away, they filled the air with melodious music. Two butterflies danced across the awakening market as vendors set up for a day of commerce.

Simon Roth stepped from his bakery, a wide smile across his face. Hefting the large package in his arms, he paused for a moment and took in the sights and sounds of his beloved piece of the world. He closed his eyes and felt the warmth of the sun wash over him as birdsong filled his ears. In the distance, the innocent giggling of children playing added their harmony to this divine morning.

He exhaled, feeling his whole body relax. He had been waiting for this day for quite a while. Market Day, the first one of the season, and this one was going to be the best one ever.

He breathed in slow and deep, catching the scent of wild flowers and spring blossoms in the air. They were followed closely by a wave of fresh baked golden buttery deliciousness from the large wrapped package he held in his hands.

This was it! He'd spent months perfecting it. Getting the exact right mix of ingredients: two sacks of flour, a gallon of buttermilk, and an entire slab of Amish butter, melted and gently basted on as it baked. It was layered, so that the scent would emanate as it cooled and fill the market with mouthwatering allure, leading the shoppers by their noses, right to his door!

His grin widened as he set his cherished masterpiece on the display table he'd made to hold it. He peeled back the layers of cheesecloth he'd wrapped it in after removing it from the oven, a warm waft of heaven washed over him. He stared down at his creation. Measuring just over twenty-four inches around, fifteen inches tall and, for all its ingredients, as light as a cloud: the perfect, giant biscuit.

Scrumptious tendrils drifted up and away, mixing with the fresh spring air and sending their invitation aloft. The affect as it reached the arriving market patrons was almost instantaneous. They sniffed at the air, perking up and looking around, searching.

The baker beamed! Customers often told him when they entered his shop and smelled all the fresh baked goodness, that if he could just pump that delightful scent outside, his shop would have a line down the block.

An elderly couple standing next to a flower vendor shifted their attention and the man pointed toward Simon. He licked his lips, grabbed his wife's hand and stepped away from the flowers, coming in the baker's direction.

Simon adjusted the sign hanging from the table that read, 'Fresh Baked Wholesome Goodness Inside! C'mon in!' and darted back in the door.

"Get ready boys," he said to the two young neighborhood kids he'd hired to help on market Saturdays. "Here they come!"

And come they did. After the elderly couple entered, the little bell that rang each time the door opened, clanged like a 5-alarm fire until the door was held open by the line stretching out of it. Simon floated around the bakery, chatting with his customers and cheering the boys on as they hustled and bustled to help the throngs of customers select their treats. He patted Timothy on the back of the shoulders and said, "What a success my biscuit is!"

Outside, the scent of the succulent biscuit aroused appetites in all who caught a whiff. One person in particular found his appetite stimulated by it in ways it hadn't been in some time. His name was Eddy, often referred to as Crazy Eddy but, unlike the many patrons of Roth's Bakery, he didn't join the line to enter the store and make a purchase.

Eddy peered from around the corner of a dark alley three buildings down. His clothes were two sizes too big and covered in the dirt and grime that came from sleeping next to a restaurant dumpster. Anyone who got close to him would've found the scent of the biscuit over-ridden by the stink emanating from the homeless man.

He sniffed at the air, hand gripping the bricks until his knuckles turned white. A strand of drool hung from his chapped lips and his sore-covered tongue darted out to catch it. Too late, the drool dripped onto the front of his stained Nirvana t-shirt. His bugged out eyes traced the round luscious curves of the giant biscuit, imagining what it felt like, how warm and moist it would be. He wanted it, wanted it bad, unlike anything he'd ever wanted before, including the drugs that had led him to his life on the streets. The thought of taking it, making it his own, consumed his mind like a demon taking possession.

A tap on his shoulder startled him out of his lusting for the biscuit. Behind him, Tyler 'Pigpen' Tulips mirrored his own hunger. They smiled at each other with wicked intent.

Inside the store, Simon hummed as he worked, thinking how he would need an extra pair of hands to help with baking even more goodies next Saturday! If business kept up at this pace, he'd be sold out before lunchtime. Everyone in the store smiled and chatted with each other in jubilant celebration. They were happy and this made Simon happy.

Then a hush came from outside the store and rolled like falling dominoes through the line to the counter. Everyone, including Simon, looked up and outside to see what had brought on this change in energy.

A dark shape darted in front of the store window, paused in front of the giant biscuit, glanced up with a wild grin and locked eyes with the baker. Then, the homeless man scooped it up and ran back the way he'd come.

A shocked cry escaped the collected onlookers as they watched him run and disappear, then all eyes turned to Simon to see what he would do.

Simon blinked. Had he really just seen someone run off with his masterpiece? His face went ghost pale as his stomach churned, then a rush came over him as the blood thundered in his veins and his cheeks turned crimson.

Someone in the line cried, "Call the police!"

Another said, "What an asshole, I'd go kick his ass."

"Yeah, I can't believe that," someone else encouraged.

Matt, one of the baker's hired hands asked, "Simon, what're you gonna do?"

Simon's fists clenched and unclenched. That man had stolen his treasure, his masterpiece. How dare he!

Simon reached up and undid the tie on his apron with a quick pull, undoing it and sliding it off in one motion. Slamming it down on the counter, he looked at the faces in the waiting line as he came around from the back. They cheered him on.

"Get him!"

"Teach him a lesson."

"Good for nothing."

"Bum!"

This last word stopped Simon in his tracks, right in the doorway. The man he'd seen grab the biscuit, he'd seen him before around the market square. He was a bum, well, homeless for sure. Homeless and hungry. Everyone had a story for how they got to where they were and Simon knew only too well how precarious keeping modern life together could be. It only took losing your minimum wage job to plunge you into poverty, and then onto the streets.

A man in line right next to Simon smacked him on the shoulder. "Get that thief!"

Simon looked at the man and then up and down the line of waiting, expectant customers. Each face bore anger, disgust, hate. They all wanted him to go after the man, to punish him. He could feel the mob energy taking hold as more and more voices spoke up with violent intent.

He took a deep breath and held it in. He'd slaved all winter to perfect the mouth watering recipe for his giant biscuit; all in order to fill his store with customers. It had worked and there they were, buying him out of everything he had baked. It was a good day for Simon Roth, perhaps the best day in his life, definitely his best day as a baker. He made a decision to not tarnish that.

"Thank you everyone. I appreciate your support today as customers and for your anger at what just happened. I'm angry too." He took a moment and looked up and down the line. "But, I also recognize that the man who just stole my biscuit is homeless and likely hungry. Who knows when he last ate. I'd planned on donating the biscuit after closing to the shelter across town."

Grimaces of anger turned soft, cold stares warmed and mad mouths gently closed.

"I'm gonna go find that man," Simon continued, "and tell him he doesn't need to steal to eat. That he can have the biscuit and, in fact, he can have it every Saturday after the market closes." A small smile formed on his lips. Yes! That was the answer. Not anger, but compassion.

Like a gentle rain, clapping started. First inside the store and then throughout the line. The customers grinned and cheered him on.

"You're a good man!"

"How charitable!"

Simon Roth's smile returned to its former size, perhaps, bigger and better than it had ever been. He left the store and headed in the direction the homeless man had fled.

II. Back Alley Biscuit

Simon walked down the street, beaming as waves of joy surged through him. He laughed out loud, from folly to fortune all in a matter of heartbeats. What a day! His big beautiful biscuit was a bigger success then he could ever have imagined.

Not only had it packed his store with customers, it had given him an opportunity to do something for others. To feed some of the hungry souls that roamed the streets of this good town and to show people there was another option besides violence and anger. Wouldn't it be great for the man who stole it to know he didn't have to be filled with guilt and shame, that his hunger could be satisfied?

Simon took in a deep breath as he neared the corner of the alley. He smelled the fragrant cherry blossoms that lined the park, the scent of his warm buttery biscuit that had so recently passed that way and then... his nose twitched. Filth.

The pungent odor of dirt, decay and garbage overwhelmed everything else. He stood at the corner, peering down into the dim alley, filled with overflowing and over-used dumpsters. The stench was sickening, but over it all, he could still smell a hint of his biscuit and, down near the far end of the alley, he saw the man who had taken it.

The man and a few others disappeared around a corner into a connecting alley. Simon paused for a moment. This probably wasn't the safest idea he'd ever had. Sure, he had good news for the man and his friends, but what if they didn't believe him? What if they thought he'd come to punish them? What if they turned on him?

A knot formed in his stomach and he realized he wasn't breathing. He took another breath of the foul air and shook his head. No. This was a good day. This would all turn out fine. He'd find them and they'd all be stuffing themselves and enjoying his biscuit and he'd let them know it'll all be okay.

He marched forward, confident and certain, only hoping he'd catch up with them before they exited the other side of the alley.

Simon approached the corner they'd disappeared around, slowing as he heard voices. Well, not only voices, but grunting and thrashing, obscenities flying. Simon's face paled, this wasn't good. They were fighting over his biscuit. What if they attacked him? He'd heard about this kind of thing on the news a few years back, a website where homeless men were paid to beat each other senseless for money. Were they killing each other over his biscuit? He took a deep breath, breathing the fear out and touching his anger once again.

He'd been up at 4am to start baking and had spent over two hours basting each layer and getting things ready. The whole point of the biscuit was to attract customers from the market with its luscious seductive scent, to make their mouths water and tickle their tummies, but this was a bit much. Hopefully they wouldn't make this a difficult conversation.

He took a deep breath, put a smile on his face and started formulating the words he wanted to say as he bent his ear to the corner. Oh my, they really seemed to be enjoying it and there were a lot of them, from the sounds of things. Maybe this wouldn't be such a difficult conversation after all. They'd be able to figure this out.

Voices carried shouts and cheers, showing exactly how much they were enjoying it.

"Give me some! That looks good."

"Mmm, that's one hot biscuit."

With his wide friendly smile pasted on, Simon stepped around the corner.

He stared. His eyes widened. His mouth fell open.

About a dozen dirty and disheveled looking men stood around a large wooden spool, once used to transport large utility cables, but now being used as a makeshift table top. The biscuit, his biscuit, steam rising off of it as it released its buttery delicious scent, sat atop the spool, its golden brown curves hugging the edges. Four or five of the men were close in, the others waiting their turn.

The men closest were… his brain stumbled, tripped, and fell down completely.

He blinked, trying to refresh the image into something he recognized. The sides of his wide open mouthed grin trembled.

He blinked again and when the image before him didn't change, he realized it was familiar after all. He'd seen images like this before. Alone in his office, with the door closed, eyes glued to a computer monitor, making his 'special' batter as he sometimes joked to himself. He'd watched porn that was a lot like this but… his brain stumbled as it tried to get up.

That was supposed to be a woman.

The noises coming from the group of men, moans and groans as they thrusted, pants down around their ankles, slammed into Simon's consciousness.

He watched one man tear a chunk of golden flakey crust free as he made his orgasm face, shouted, "Oh yeah!" and stepped away, allowing the next disheveled looking man to step up and take his turn.

"Get in there while she's still hot," the first man encouraged the second.

Simon watched as the man grabbed hold of the makeshift table, shoulder to shoulder with the others, made a fresh hole and proceeded to…

Simon's mind fell down again. Face-plant. He felt a strange twitch in his groin and then a revolt in his stomach. He stumbled back around the corner, still grinning. The smile was now frozen on his face in a Joker like plastic surgery gone wrong kinda way, and he fell to his knees and retched.

Like an erupting volcano, turned upside down, the undigested quiche he'd eaten just before opening rained down. Chunks of egg, spinach and feta cheese, steamed on the pavement like a Rorschach blot. His stomach twisted, causing his knees to weaken and another wave released from inside of him as he sunk down to the concrete, one hand on the wall holding him steady. The voices of the men, enjoying themselves, drifted over him between expulsions.

"I like it when they just lay there and take it."

"This gives new meaning to fresh baked goodness."

"I want in before it cools off."

"I like it when they struggle!"

"Don't worry, my hot load will keep it warm for you."

Wishing he'd left his apron on, Simon wiped away the strands hanging from his mouth with the back of his hand. His stomach lurched again, but nothing came up.

Those sick bastards. How dare they do that with... *his biscuit.* He was dry heaving now, tears staining his cheeks, but the smile, the crazy, won't-go-away smile, stayed put.

The voices from around the corner carried on.

"Uhh, uhh."

"Our little back alley biscuit."

"Yeah!"

Cries of pleasure, lust and release floated into his ears as he quietly heaved, the muscles of his stomach aching.

He peeked up and around the corner, still not wanting to believe what he knew was reality. The man who'd stolen it backed away, his cock long and limp, covered in crumbs. His beautiful biscuit's crumbs.

Before the thief even had a chance to pull up his pants, another man stepped from the shadows and took his place. His dick already out, it was crooked and hard. He'd been watching and stroking himself while the other men raped... the biscuit.

Despair washed over Simon as streams of tears mixed with the strings of upchuck hanging from his cheeks.

How could they? What kind of animals would do something like that? His questions turned to curses. Those sick fuckers. How dare they defile something so wholesome, so full of love. He wanted to shout, to scream at them, make them stop, but he found himself paralyzed. Shock held him captive and he watched as man after man took turns on his sweet biscuit.

Pieces had fallen off now, large chunks lay on the ground next to the spindle and the center of the biscuit had sunk. The men, those fucking bastards, laughed and joked with one another.

"I'm gonna butter this biscuit!"

"Yeah, well, I'm gonna make this thing juicier than a jelly donut."

Then slowly, one by one, they started to leave, heading out the other side of the alley. Simon knew he either needed to stand up and shout, or run. He climbed to his feet. I can do this, I can do this. Then he noticed that strange twitch in his groin had turned into an erection. His boner stuck out, popping a tent in his pants. His cheeks went red. What the fuck was this? He couldn't berate these men for what they had just done with his dick sticking out like that.

He saw the man who'd stolen the biscuit and another walk over to the makeshift table and examine the remains. They laughed and joked.

"That was almost like the real thing," the thief said.

"I hope he bakes another one of these little bitch biscuits next Saturday," the other replied.

"C'mon," the thief said, grabbing the sides of the giant empty spool, "let's get rid of the evidence."

They hefted the table and carried it over to one of the dumpsters and tilted it until the cum-filled biscuit slid off and disappeared with a thunk.

"Just like dead hooker storage," the thief laughed.

This last comment caused Simon's brain to freeze in fear. His stomach lurched again, but with nothing in it, it just made his wide, crazy smile flex a little. He backed away, scared that if they saw him, they might add his body to the dumpster. He didn't think the world would be ready for that headline.

'Local Baker Found in Dumpster with Semen Filled Biscuit'

He slipped into an alcove behind a restaurant that didn't open until lunchtime and waited. He breathed and tried in, trying to calm his racing heart. His erection, much like his smile, still raged on, stuck in position. One of the men walked past Simon, he wasn't sure which one, as he kept his face turned into the darkness. After a while, when he was sure they had all departed, he stepped from the shadows and made his way back to where the men had been.

The alley was littered with pieces of brown flaky crust, crumbs strewn everywhere. He walked to the dumpster and looked inside.

The biscuit lay, smashed and ruined at the bottom. He could see the unnatural ingredient the men had added to it, and it wasn't healthy. It was thick and yellow and there were red and black spots in some of it.

He retched again.

They didn't eat any of it. They just used it, they used his sweet buttery biscuit like it was... was a...

His mind collapsed again.

It went through a few cycles trying to reboot as he stared at the scattered remains of his biscuit. When he finally came back online, the mad grin he wore shrank just enough to not be too wide, but still wide enough to give someone the creeps if they looked at him too long or tried to have a conversation with him.

He walked robot like back out of the alley and down the sidewalk, not even trying to hide the erection that protruded from his pants. He entered the bakery to a torrent of questions from the customers, to which he just continued to smile and walked past them. No one, except one of his employees noticed the erection, as they were all to focused on his smile and wondering why he didn't say anything.

He went behind the counter, slipped into the back and entered his office, closing the door. A moment later, he had his computer booted up, his pants down around his ankles and found himself on that website he'd heard about on the news, but never visited. The action of homeless men beating each other up on his screen played out as Simon beat out his special batter.

"It's time for a new recipe," he repeated with each stroke.

III. A Recipe For Love

The bakery was closed on Sundays and Simon did

not open it on Monday morning either. He emerged from his office in the late afternoon, unshaven, eyes and palms red, still smiling his demented smile, revenge on his mind. He needed help and he knew just the person to do so. Her name was Kumin Lerot, an ancient Asian woman who had space in the back of a shop in Chinatown.

He'd been referred to her when he was in culinary school and in need of a special ingredient. While it hadn't worked out quite as he had hoped, her special ingredient had done what it was supposed to.

At first it was something of a lark, but he figured he could use all the help he could get. He had a date with Amber Fitzgerald, a stunning blonde, whose family was from the upper east side. Way out of his league, but somehow he'd gotten her to say yes to a date. She was in meteorology school, training to be a future weather woman.

He was a first year chef. He had overheard Amber one day in the cafeteria talking about how she hadn't had a gourmet meal since she'd left home. He spoke up, saying, "I'm a chef. I'll cook a meal you'll never forget." This was both uncharacteristically bold for Simon, as well as mostly untrue. He'd only been in culinary school for a few months, but he did have some skills to work with.

She'd given him a look of disbelief that he'd even dare speak to her, let alone ask her out on a date, when her stomach rumbled. They both laughed and her smile had captivated him. "Ok," she'd said, "You get one chance to wow me." He'd beamed and scribbled his address down; a loft he shared with four other students and a bulldog named Max.

He had spent the rest of the week practicing making the best meal he could in the school's kitchens.

One day one of his instructors, an older gay man, had asked him what he was so busy trying to accomplish. When he'd finished explaining the story, the old chef laughed and said, "Sounds like you'll be needing some special ingredients."

"What do you mean?" Simon had asked.

"You need a love potion!"

"What?"

The man had smiled. "I know, sounds crazy, but when you've been in the culinary arts as long as I have, you come to learn a few things. How certain ingredients can make not only a difference in taste, but also how they react within the body."

Simon shook his head, "So you know a recipe that'll make her fall in love with me?"

"No, not a recipe," the old chef said, "but an ingredient and where to find it. There's this old woman in Chinatown…"

That night Simon had ventured to the location he'd been given. He'd met the woman, Kumin Lerot and her grandson, Thomas. She'd given him what he needed and, through her grandson had said, "I have ingredients to help you with whatever troubles you might have, friends, lovers, even enemies."

At the time, this last bit had creeped him out, but he

wasn't really sure any of it was real, but he was willing to take any chance he could to win Amber's heart.

It would've worked too… if things hadn't gone terribly wrong.

When the night for their date arrived, Simon had everything ready to make a wonderful gourmet meal. Herb crusted halibut in a butter cream piccata sauce, with wild rice and fresh steamed asparagus - and he'd even gotten all of his roommates out of the house for the night. That had only left the chubby bulldog as a potential problem, but he planned to feed him a hefty meal and lock him in one of the bedrooms to sleep it off.

Max lay on the couch in the living room, watching as Simon hummed and danced around the kitchen, dabbing at his brow with a towel to wipe the sweat away.

Simon ground up the dried root Kumin had sold him, and let it simmer into the sauce. It smelled a bit like nutmeg, he thought. He continued dancing around the kitchen, he couldn't believe he would soon have Amber Fitzgerald in his apartment. He glanced at the clock, ten to seven, she'd arrive any minute!

"Come eat, Max!"

He poured a large bowl of kibble and waited expectantly as the dog lumbered over, sniffed at the food, then sat and stared at Simon. Like his roommates, none of which were good cooks, Max had come to expect a little more from Simon than just plain food.

"C'mon Max, eat up!"

The dog just stared at him.

"Don't make me put you to bed without dinner." The last bit was an empty threat, as Simon knew all too well that a Max with an empty belly was a Max that would be whining and barking all night, and that would not make for a good date.

Simon turned back to his preparations, spreading some of the sauce on to the plates, creating a bed for the halibut to rest in and making sure that each bite would be coated with the special ingredient on all sides.

Max sniffed at the air as he spooned the mixture on the plates.

Simon chuckled. "No, no boy, that's not for you. Now eat."

Max continued to not eat, switching his gaze from Simon to the simmering sauce pan on the stove.

Simon checked the oven, the halibut would be ready in a few minutes. A glance at the clock read 6:55pm, Amber would arrive at— knock, knock!

Shit!

He'd hoped to have Max put away before she got there. "C'mon boy, let's go." Simon picked up the dog's food bowl and headed toward Richard's room. Max just sat, staring at the stove where the sauce simmered.

Simon walked back, fully intending to pick up the 80lb bulldog and carry him and the food to the bedroom, when another, slightly more insistent knock jarred his nerves. He rushed to the kitchen and heaped a spoonful of the sauce onto the dog's food, stirred it and, as Max got to his feet, Simon shook his head. "You're insufferable."

He headed to the bedroom with Max close on his heels. He put him inside, set the food down and closed the door, then ran to the front door right as a very curt third knocking started.

"Hi!" He opened the door with the biggest smile he could muster. "Sorry, I was trying to make everything... purrr...fect!" He stumbled over his words as he looked her up and down.

She wore a slinky blue dress that clung tight to the curves of her hips, ending just above the knees. The top sat off the shoulders with a plunging neckline that revealed her naturally pert breasts, tanned and ripe, like melons on display. She looked ready for a night on the town, not dinner in a loft.

"You look absolutely stunning," Simon managed.

"Thank you," she said, her annoyance at being kept waiting cooling a bit with the compliment. "I felt a fancy meal deserved a fancy dress." She spun around in her matching blue heels, revealing the backless portion that dipped so low he swore he saw a hint of her crack. "You like?"

"Yes!" he shouted, spit spraying from his lips, barely missing her. "I hope you like dinner nearly as much!"

She sniffed the air. "Mmm, what is that? It smells good."

He took her hand and led her inside.

"It's halibut in a special creamy piccata sauce. Ever had it?"

"No, but I love halibut, it's my favorite fish."

She sniffed at the air again, smiling and taking a deep breath, then she sneezed hard.

"Achoo!" It knocked her head forward, tousling her hair.

"Bless you," Simon let go of her hand and rushed to the kitchen finding a clean towel and handing it to her.

"Thank you," she dabbed at her nose and looked around the space with watery eyes. "Do you have a dog?"

"No," Simon said, then, "I mean, I don't, but my roommate Richard does, he's put away in his bedroom."

"Oh." She stood a little straighter and pulled her purse strap back up over her shoulder, looking like she was getting ready to leave. "I love them, but I'm highly allergic."

Simon felt panic grip his stomach. "Here," he grabbed her hand hoping she wouldn't notice the sweat dripping from his own and walked her toward the table. "Let me get you seated and open some windows, that should help."

A fresh cool breeze flowed into the room as soon as he had them open.

"Thank you," she smiled at him as he lit two tapered candles on the table before her.

"Ok, just a couple of minutes." He walked around the counter and back into the kitchen. "Would you like some wine? I have a bottle of Pinot Grigio to go with the halibut." He stirred the sauce.

"That sounds lovely, Simon. No one's made me a

good meal since I came to school. Our family chef was amazing. School cafeteria food, not so much."

Simon bit his lip; he probably shouldn't tell her that the lunches were prepared by the culinary students then. And she had a family chef? How was he supposed to compare to that? He poured her glass a little extra full. Love potion or not, he did need all the help he could get!

He sat the glass down and said, "One gourmet meal coming right up."

She grinned at him. "Thank you Simon. That smell is making my tummy rumble even louder than the other day." She laughed at the memory. "And thank you for opening the window, it really helps."

They met each other's gazes, smiles widening and eyes twinkling.

Back in the kitchen, Simon slid the halibut onto the prepared plates. Then he ladled two heaping spoonfuls of sauce on top of each of them. Five minutes after ingesting it, the effects would kick in. Thomas had translated this information from Kumin. Whoever ate it would be filled with burning desire for the first person they saw.

Simon had to bite his tongue to keep his grin from spreading as wide as a loon. Having this golden goddess fall in love with him would be more than he could ever dream of. The thought of peeling off that tight blue dress and running his hands over her body made his slacks a little tighter.

He picked up both plates and came around the counter to the table.

"Mademoiselle, my masterpiece is served." He slid the plate in front of her and she oohed at it, then turned to smile up at him.

"That looks so delicious. Thank you, Simon."

He floated to his seat and sat down across from her.

"You really know the way to a woman's heart. Cook her an amazing meal!"

She smiled and laughed and, for a moment, Simon wished he hadn't resorted to a love potion. Maybe it wouldn't have been needed.

"Let's dig in," she said, "I could eat a horse." She picked up her fork and then stopped, her eyes narrowing.

A bark followed by whining and scratching at the bedroom door startled them both. Simon tried to ignore it and stuck his fork in the halibut anyway, but another bark followed.

"I'm sorry," he said, "he's probably just lonely. I walked him before you got here. Let me just go make sure he's alright." Simon stood and turned back, "Go ahead and eat, enjoy it while it's hot."

Amber's face softened, "You're a good man, Simon."

He glowed as he walked over to the door. He placed his hand on the knob and turned back as Amber spoke again.

"I think I'm in trouble," she said, raising a fork full of sauce covered halibut to her lips.

"Why's that?" Simon said, swinging the door open.

"You're too easy to fall for." The fork hung in the air just about to disappear behind those luscious lips.

Simon's own mouth hung open. He couldn't wait to kiss them.

Then pandemonium struck.

With the door open, the beefy bulldog had an unobstructed view of Amber. He shot out of the bedroom, ran across the living room, up onto the couch and then launched himself into the air.

Simon watched as Amber's delightful smile disappeared, turning confused, then to open mouthed fright. She dropped her fork as Max slammed onto the table, then lunged directly onto her in one leap. Plates went flying, glasses tumbled and Amber fell backward, her chair toppling as she tried to scoot away but was knocked over by Max's bulk colliding with her.

Simon couldn't see what was happening, only hearing the shouts and cries from Amber as she hit the floor, being mauled by Max. He ran to her, sounds of her dress being ripped apart tore into him. Oh, shit!

He came around the corner of the table, and saw Amber lying in the remains of the broken chair, struggling to get away from Max. Her dress was torn, exposing her breasts and hiked up to her waist, revealing she hadn't worn any panties; and atop her… Max was humping away on her chest. His claws left raw red marks on her exposed flesh and tore into the skin of her arms. He licked her cheeks, leaving long globs of slobber clinging to them.

Simon bent over and grabbed the dog, lifting him off her. Max continued to thrust, his erect penis jutting from its sheath.

"Oh my God, oh my God!" Amber cried. Her chest was a mess of criss-crossed slashes, raised and swelling. Her face too began to swell. First her cheeks then her lips, causing her cries to sound like, 'Oh ma-goo' instead of 'Oh my God.'

Simon wrestled the air humping Max onto the patio and slid the glass door closed. He turned back to Amber, who grasped at the table, her legs trembling as she pulled herself to her feet. She blubbered, spittle rolling off her swollen lips as he tried to take her hand and help her.

She slapped him away, shouting unintelligibly as she reached up and touched her face, then her chest. Her whole body was having an allergic reaction.

"Please Amber, let me help you," Simon tried.

She pushed past him, pulling the torn flap of her dress over her exposed breasts and making for the door.

Simon stood, paralyzed, watching her go.

The door slammed shut and his stomach sank. He looked around the chaos of the room. The table was demolished, with broken plates, ruined food and wine scattered from one end to the other. Just like his dreams of love ever-after. Completely destroyed.

He caught a glimpse of blue fabric amongst the carnage on the floor, bent down and picked it up. He clung to it. It was a piece of her dress, a piece that... Max! Rage filled Simon. He turned to the patio and the dog that had ruined his night. He wanted to hurt him.

On the patio, Max paced back and forth, whining and occasionally stopping to dry hump the air, his pink penis still protruding.

Simon opened the door, glowering at the dog. "You worthless mutt!"

Max ignored him and continued his panting and whining. Then a car horn went off, the kind that sounds when you unlock your car. Max perked up and bounded to the edge, looking down four stories to the street.

Simon glanced where he was looking and saw Amber making her way to her car. One last chance, he threw his arms up in the air and shouted. "Amber, please wait!"

At the same moment, Max took a few steps backward and with one quick leap, jumped onto a bench, knocked over Simon's fresh herb garden and hurtled himself over the edge of the patio, right in front of Simon.

Amber looked up, seeing Simon, arms extended and Max falling like a stone right beneath him.

Even from four stories away and with her face swollen so grotesquely she was no longer recognizable, Simon could see her horror stricken expression.

Max impacted with the concrete sidewalk only a few feet from Amber, showering her in a splattering of red rain.

She stumbled backward, tripping in her heels and slamming into the side of her car. She stared up at Simon, who still had his arms extended, looking like he had tossed Max at her. She grasped at her car door and pulled it open. "Yug hurgible!" she blustered, opened the door and disappeared. With a lurch, her car started and screeched out of its parking spot.

Simon never saw her again.

While the end result of his love potion experiment had not been what he wanted it to be, the power of it and the potential possibilities if needed had always stayed with him. Now, he once again stood outside of the little shop in Chinatown, the sign on the door advertising, 'Acupuncture, Gifts, Massage and Herbal Remedies'. Inside, he hoped Miss Lerot still resided. It was time for a new recipe.

IV. Special Ingredients

While not much from the outside, inside the shop stretched for what seemed like an entire city block. There were aisles upon aisles of merchandise with foreign writing. Jars containing strange looking things and in a couple, Simon swore he saw something moving.

He couldn't tell where they possibly did acupuncture and massage, but with as much stuff as they had in the store, he figured they had a table or two hidden somewhere. He remembered, Kumin had been in the back corner in a papasan style chair with a small drape hanging over the sides of it, shrouding her in darkness.

Before Simon could make his way to the back, a teenage boy sitting behind the front counter looked up from a television so ancient, Simon didn't even remember having one that old as a kid.

"May I help you?" the boy asked in perfect English.

The boy looked exactly like the woman's grandson

he'd met fifteen years before. That couldn't be him though. Simon dismissed the thought; it must be another family member.

"Yes," Simon answered, his lips twitching and his eyes feverish. "I'm here to see the old woman, Kumin."

The boy looked at him a moment, then nodded. "Follow me."

The boy led him down ever darkening aisles for what seemed a very long time. This made no sense to Simon since he could see light fixtures spaced equally on the low ceiling. The dimmer it grew, the cooler the air became, and Simon wished he'd brought his coat along.

As they rounded a corner, the boy stepped to one side and there she was, exactly as he remembered her. Shrouded in shadows, only her bony hands visible. One clutched a very large, very old television remote control that only had five buttons. In her other hand, a shiny black ribbon, about six inches long, was laced between her fingers. It moved, flowing across and under them like a snake as she worked it with her ancient hand.

From beside her chair, the boy motioned to a footstool before her. Simon sat as he had the last time. From this level, the woman's ancient face was visible. Though of Asian descent, her face was pale white, as if she hadn't seen the sun in decades and indeed, she may not have.

"What is it you seek?" the boy asked.

Simon glanced from the old woman to the boy, his purpose for coming surfacing. Images of the men and his biscuit flashed through his mind. He clenched his jaw, lips wrinkling together as he forced the words from his mouth. "I am in need of some special ingredients."

The boy nodded. "For what purpose?"

Simon hadn't thought about that, exactly. Only that if she could make love potions as strong as she did, perhaps her potions for enemies would be equally potent.

"I need," he paused, holding his breath, uncertain. He stared into the eyes of the old woman, her small dark pupils studying him. "A poison," Simon finally let out.

The woman spoke then, a few brief words in her native tongue.

The boy said, "She says she remembers you."

Then a few more words from the woman to the boy.

"She asks if you're here because you've grown tired of your lover?"

"No, no, it's nothing like that." Simon said in a rush. "She's long gone now."

The woman tilted her head, eyes narrowing a little. She spoke in a quick bark to her grandson.

"She asks, why she is gone? Did you follow the instructions?"

Simon nodded. "Yes, I did. It worked perfectly. I'm not here because of that. I am here because I thought she could help me with another situation."

The boy spoke to the old woman for a moment and she answered with a grunt.

"Explain," said the boy.

Simon took a breath and let the words rush out of

him. "I'm a baker. I have a shop near Camden Circle, where the Saturday Market is. I created a recipe for a giant biscuit. It's a thing of golden, mouth-watering, nose enchanting beauty. I placed it outside my shop so that its sight and scent would attract people from the marketplace. Only…"

He paused for a moment while the boy translated for the woman.

"Shortly after I put it out, a homeless man stole it and ran off with it." He debated saying more, but instead, just added, "I want to stop him."

The boy translated again and she nodded, looking at Simon with a tilted head and squinting eyes. She spoke three sharp words and then the boy turned back to Simon.

"Poison seems a harsh punishment for simple thievery."

It's not thievery, it's buggery! Simon wanted to yell. His face scrunched as he tried to keep the crazed smile that had plagued him since the incident in the alley from creeping out. He sat on the stool, rocking himself back and forth as images of the homeless men gang-raping his biscuit raged through his mind. The corners of his lips declared victory over his sanity and twisted upward. Before he even realized it, he was telling the story of what he had seen as he rocked on the stool. The words flowed out in a machine gun-like staccato, rapid fire, spit flying bursts. As he ranted, he saw the old woman reach out and grab a small empty jar from a shelf next to her. It disappeared within her robes and she too began to rock back and forth in unison with him.

He told the whole tale, ending with the ruined biscuit lying, broken and used, in the dumpster. He found that he was panting, short of breath, staring at the floor, a little blurry eyed. He looked up as a cool damp hand touched his own.

The old woman leaned forward, her face just inches from his. She wore a wide grin, revealing many missing teeth. Her other hand contained the jar, now full of a white creamy mixture that looked like spoiled milk. She handed it to the boy as she squeezed Simon's hand and spoke two words.

"Gully worms," she cackled, and slid back into the darkness of her chair.

Simon looked at the boy, who as far as he recalled hadn't translated a word of what he'd just said. The boy tilted his head toward the front of the store and walked away. Simon glanced at the woman once more, seeing in the darkness only the white of her still wide, missing-toothed grin.

Back at the front counter, the boy set the jar down, placed a lid on it and sealed it. He turned to a small sink, reached underneath and pulled out a bottle marked 'bleach'. He proceeded to pour some of the liquid directly onto his hands and then washed under the faucet with soap and water. After drying, he walked back to where Simon waited. "Don't get any on you," he said, and then started pressing buttons on an ancient cash register.

"What are 'Gully Worms'?" Simon asked, "and how do I use them?"

"$5000," the boy said in reply.

Simon's eyes widened and his lips parted. That's almost my entire credit line, he thought. He was about to protest, then the image of his ruined masterpiece, laying broken, used and uneaten in the dumpster overrode any objection. He pulled out his wallet and handed over his credit card.

The boy swiped it through the machine and watched the small screen until the word 'Approved' showed, then he spoke. "They are not really worms, that is just their name. They are more like a larvae. They were most often used in the old country to protect women during times of war and occasionally to punish a cheating spouse."

Simon watched as the receipt printed out of the credit card terminal, was torn free and set before him along with a pen. He stared down at the amount.

"They place them inside," the boy shuddered at this, "and when a man enters them…"

The boy stopped there and Simon looked up from the receipt waiting.

"So how do *I* use them?"

"Make your biscuit," the boy answered, "slice off the top, make a hollow in the center and pour these in. The heat and warmth will awaken them."

Again, the boy stopped, leaving Simon waiting.

"What happens?"

The boy scrunched up his face and shook off a shiver

that ran through his body. "It is most unpleasant. Have you ever heard stories of a wound infected with larvae from a fly? Maggots fill the space and eventually turn to flies... and leave." The boy stared into Simon's eyes. "It's like that, only these larvae have teeth."

Simon's smile flexed with glee.

"They are tiny at first," the boy continued. "Then they get restless and start eating. They get bigger. It'll be like a warm itching sensation that grows more and more uncomfortable."

Simon unconsciously reached down and adjusted his cock in his pants.

"They'll hollow out the shaft, eating everything, until they are trapped inside the skin. This happens very quickly. It will look like a bloated moving sausage as the larvae wriggle. After they've run out of things to eat, they will begin eating each other. Their soft spiked vertebrate will harden as they ingest a special protein from their brethren, forming an armored carapace that will rip through the flesh of the victim and leave it a flaccid tattered ruin."

The boy stopped there as Simon, all smiles, picked up the pen and signed without another thought.

He whistled as he left the store.

V. The Baker's New Recipe

Bluebirds and robins chirped their sing-song melody in the morning sun. The scent of spring flowers filled the air. Kids played in the park. Joggers ran along the sidewalks. In the market center, vendors set up their booths.

A small bell chimed as the door to Roth's Bakery opened and the baker carried his main attraction out to the display table at the entrance. A simple, satisfied smile rested on his lips as he set it down, unwrapped it, and watched the delicious tendrils of steam waft into the air, sending their beckoning delight out to the crowds.

Today, the biscuit loves back!

- END

To learn more about the author, Grivante, find his author bio at http://www.grivantepress.com/

BURNT SCRAMBLED EGGS
By Devon Widmer

After fishing a wedgie out of her crack, Tammy sighed into the musty refrigerator air. Her midnight snack options were limited to a jar of expired mayonnaise, half a carton of cracked eggs, and a solitary pickle swimming in its juices. Grimacing, she grabbed the pickle jar. But before she could unscrew the top, a puff of cold air tickled the nape of her neck. Startled, she whipped around to face... her empty kitchen.

Back in bed, Tammy savored the combined taste of pickles and toothpaste—*Delicious*. She folded her hands behind her head. Nothing like getting laid off from the once-in-a-lifetime-shot-at-success-in-the-big-city dream job to really bring on the insomnia. Exactly how much longer would she be able to scrape by before she had to slink back to her parents' house with her tail between her legs like a chicken?

Wait. Did that even make sense? Tammy rubbed her palms against her eyes and yawned. She *seriously* needed some sleep. Closing her eyes, she conjured a herd of fluffy white sheep milling along the back of her eyelids. *One sheep, two sheep, I want, to sleep…*

Creeeeaaaak.

"Who's there?" Tammy bolted upright—the gravely groan of her bedroom door opening had sent those imaginary sheep running for the imaginary hills. She blinked frantically to bring the dark room into focus. *Strange.* Her bedroom door was still shut.

Her eyes rolled back in frustration, Tammy drug her fingertips down her cheeks. She'd been spooking herself all night, jumping at every moan of the wind or creak of her upstairs neighbors' floorboards. It was kinda funny, really. She forced out a loud, "Ha!" and aimed a pair of finger pistols at the offending door. "Nice one, apartment." She clicked her tongue twice as if firing. "Almost had me there." Then, after flopping back down onto the bed, she pulled the covers all the way up to her nose.

Tammy's eyes flitted groggily open. A heavy pressure had settled onto her chest. Breathing shallowly, she tried to sit up but her body refused to respond. Instead, she simply lay limp, gaze immovably fixed on the whirring blades of her ceiling fan.

She'd had dreams like this before, lying in bed, unable to move, asleep but not asleep. It would pass. And hey, at least she was finally getting some rest.

It was hard to feel restful, however, when clacking footsteps, like a dog long overdue for a nail trim, began meandering around the room, halting at last at the foot of the bed. Tammy's heart raced as the sheets slipped smoothly down her body, settling into a crumpled pile by her feet. She shivered. If she'd known freaky dream monsters would be stealing her covers, she'd have worn more than a nightshirt and panties to bed.

Two clawed fingers glided into view. *It's just a dream. It's just a dream.* Tammy chanted the mantra in her head as the jagged fingertips hovered inches above her eyeballs. She'd had some frightening dreams in her time, but this felt awfully *real.* The claws descended. After planting firmly on Tammy's forehead, they slid down, forcibly closing her eyelids.

A cool breeze caressed Tammy's cheeks and the exposed bit of tummy peeking out from her misbuttoned nightshirt. Inhaling the aroma of freshly cut grass, she watched fat clouds drift lazily through a blue sky. Tammy couldn't recall how she had gotten here, but this place was nice—and oddly familiar.

"Hey there, beautiful."

Tammy glanced over.

A woman in a billowing white dress lounged next to her. The woman's chin rested delicately on the back of one hand while the other combed casually through her long blond hair. "Wanna like, do it, or whatever?" Her full red lips stretched into a smile.

"Excuse me?"

"You. Me. The big S-E-X." The woman threw her

shoulders back in a blatant attempt to showcase her unrealistically-perky-for-their-size boobs. "Isn't this, like, one of your fantasies or something? Getting seduced by a voluptuous woman in broad daylight at the top of Hookup Hill?"

Furrowing her brow, Tammy sat up for a better look at her surroundings. So that's why this place felt familiar. This *was* Hookup Hill, the official unofficial make-out destination overlooking her hometown high school football stadium. She *had* fantasized about this. "Guess I always imagined the seductress a bit more…"

"What? Tall? Dark? Buff?" In the blink of an eye, the woman morphed into a raven-haired Amazon with chiseled biceps.

Tammy's mouth drooped in disbelief—until it clicked. *Duh.* The sleep-paralysis, the monster in her bedroom… *this was all still a dream.* After snapping her mouth shut, Tammy did her best impression of a cheeky grin and responded, "… suave."

"Oh." The pouty blonde rematerialized. She scrunched her face like she was sucking on a lemon. "Mmm-K," she said at last, "got it." She batted her eyelashes. "Did it hurt?"

"Uh, did what hurt?"

"When you displeased the Almighty and had your ass booted out of heaven—you know, cause your beauty's akin to a fallen angel or whatever." When Tammy's only response was a slight grimace, Blondie scowled and puffed out her cheeks. "Can we just skip to the sex already. I'm actually *good* at the sex."

Tammy blushed but couldn't help eyeing Blondie's temptingly plump lips. *Screw it.* This was all just a dream. What was the harm in having a little fun? "I guess a kiss would be ok."

Blondie peeled those lips back into a smirk. "Sorry, hot stuff, no can do. You only get one kiss and it comes last —well, only one kiss on the lips at least. I could always kiss you... elsewhere."

"So, like on the cheek?"

"Not exactly what I had in mind," said Blondie with a throaty chuckle, "but sure, why not?" She cupped Tammy's face in her hands and, leaning in, planted a wet kiss on each of Tammy's cheeks. After pulling back to admire her sloppy handiwork, Blondie slung her arms over Tammy's shoulders. "Now, let's lose the clothes." She slithered her hands down to rest on the top button of Tammy's pajama shirt. "Whataya say?"

Tammy fidgeted with her shirttail before shyly meeting Blondie's gaze. Then, jutting out her chin, she gave an assertive nod. "Go for it." While Blondie's delicate fingers unbuttoned her nightshirt, Tammy attempted a sexy smolder. But as she squinted, Blondie's face blurred: her mouth elongated into a gaping maw with curved fangs erupting from either side, her eyes glowed red and her hair coiled into two spiraled horns.

"Something wrong?"

Trembling, Tammy blinked a few times. Blondie's eyes, safely blue again, examined her inquisitively.

"Nothing," said Tammy, shaking her head. The motion caused her unbuttoned nightshirt to slip off her shoulders. "J-just a tad cold."

"I can tell." Blondie grinned at Tammy's exposed breasts. "Mind if I warm you up?" She held up her hands and clenched her fingers hungrily.

Under the guidance of Blondie's deft fingers and darting tongue, the gruesome visage Tammy had witnessed easily slipped from her mind.

"Ready for that kiss?"

Practically panting, Tammy whispered, "Damn right I am."

After carefully un-entwining two pairs of sweaty limbs, Blondie straddled Tammy's waist. Leaning down, she sucked Tammy's lower lip into her mouth and gently chewed. Then, she traced her tongue to Tammy's earlobe. "Sure you want it?" When Tammy nodded, she added, "Fair warning, it comes with a cost."

"A cost?" Tammy furrowed her brow. She hadn't realized this was *that* kind of encounter. "How much?"

Blondie's lips curled back into a wickedly toothy smile. "About five years, give or take."

"Haha, what?" As beads of sweat stung Tammy's eyes, she couldn't help but note the predatory glint in Blondie's eyes.

"One kiss. Five years of your life. Your call."

Tammy grinned and swept the sweat from her eyes. Five years? What a bizarre joke. And what a bizarre—but amusing—way to end a session of lovemaking. She dug her fingernails into Blondie's back. "Just fucking kiss me already."

As Blondie's hungry lips locked on her own, Tammy felt her whole body shudder, as if the very breath was being sucked from her lungs.

Brrr! Brrr! Brrr!

Tammy flapped a hand onto her bedside table, fumbling for her alarm clock. But no matter how many times she punched the "off" button, the annoying *Brrr!* persisted.

Then the smell of smoke registered. *Fire? Fire!*

In a panic of flailing arms and legs, Tammy tumbled out of bed. After unsuckering her face from the floorboards, she crawled toward the bedroom door. But before she could reach for the knob, the door burst open. A wall of smoke stung Tammy's eyes. Choking down thick air, she squinted. A pair of clawed feet cut through the smoke, darting past.

Tammy rolled over just in time to see a blurry figure throw open her bedroom window. Slowly, the smoke cleared. "Holy shit," Tammy murmured. Silhouetted by the soft morning light was the horned monster from her nightmare.

The monster coughed and then tucked a few scorched strands of purple hair behind her ear. "Sorry bout that," she said, her fanged underbite muffling her words.

Tammy's mouth flapped open and closed a few

times but not a single word made its way out.

Brrr! Brrr! Brrr!

With a growl, the monster strode from the room. The fire alarm only managed one more *Brr*— before it was silenced by a plaster-cracking rip.

Her head whirling from smoke inhalation and shock, Tammy wobbled to her feet before collapsing onto her bed. Her eyes locked onto the open door. No way was that monster real. She was probably just still dreaming. When several sharp pinches failed to reset this freakish morning, Tammy covered her whole face with her hands and rubbed her forehead. Dream or not, she was in some serious shit.

"Yeah, so, I went ahead and made you breakfast." The monster reentered, a cracked plate clutched in her talons.

Tammy stared dumbly as she accepted the offering: a steaming pile of charred eggs?

"We're not really supposed to do stuff like that but I'm like, a rule breaker or whatever. Plus it just seems like the polite thing to do, ya know? Especially after a night like last night." Horny McFangface, who Tammy was beginning to accept was not simply a dream, winked.

"So you're saying last night really happened?" Tammy wrinkled her nose at the aroma of the burnt scrambled eggs. "I actually did it with a what are you exactly?"

"Succubus. And yeah, last night really happened. Though the whole blonde tart on the grassy hill scenario was a bit of a…"

"Sham? Hallucination? Blatant lie?"

"... tweaking of reality. Now, eat. I know you're feeling—what's that thing human's always complain about?—tired? After all, I did drain like five years off your lifespan."

The fork clattered to the floor as Tammy dropped the plate of scrambled eggs onto her lap. "*What?!*"

"Yeah, it was pretty awesome." Horny raised a clawed hand like she expected a high five.

"What. The. Hell. You *shortened my lifespan?* Seriously. What the hell?"

"I did warn you." Horny looked genuinely befuddled, as if Tammy ought to have been congratulating her on a successful conquest rather than trembling with anger. "Besides, it's only a handful of years. So you'll die a seventy-nine instead of eighty-four. Big whoop. That's still like, better than the average human."

Tammy's jaw dropped. "You know when I'm gonna die." Exasperated, she fell backward onto the bed, arms sprawled. "You know when I'm gonna die, and you decided to make it happen sooner?"

"Just what I do, sweetheart." Horny's face loomed into view above Tammy. Her lips, now a pinkish purple, tightened into an oddly enchanting pucker. "Enjoy the eggs—I'd kiss you goodbye, but I've a feeling you're not willing to pay the price." Horny winked before slipping from view.

"Hold it right there," said Tammy, snapping upright. She crossed her arms tightly against her chest and scowled. "I guess a kiss on the cheek would be acceptable—

provided *those* still come free."

Horny cocked her head to one side before breaking out into an infuriatingly infectious bout of laughter. "For you, tender tits, no charge." Tammy made a purposeful show of rolling her eyes as Horny kissed her three times—a peck on each cheek and a final sloppy smooch on her forehead.

Later, after Horny had vanished in a flourish of sizzling flames, Tammy relaxed her arms. She retrieved the fallen fork, speared a chunk of burnt scrambled eggs and took a bite. She chewed carefully and then swallowed. Surprisingly not bad. Good even. Not five-years-of-her-life good. But still—the hint of a smile played on her lips as she shoveled another forkful into her mouth—pretty darn good.

-END

To learn more about the author, Devon Widmer, find her author bio at http://www.grivantepress.com/

THE DISAGREEABLE DINNER
By Mark Daponte

Will Fasso walked into his kitchen to see his wife, Susan, wearing a bathrobe, a long face and bags under her blue eyes. He opened the curtains to let sunlight in and noticed that their local TV weatherman was finally right.

"Look! It really *did* snow three feet last night!" Will exclaimed. "Hurray! Now we won't have to go and visit your parents!"

"You know the roads will be cleared by the afternoon."

"Unfortunately, I do know. We'll dig the car out after breakfast."

"I'm way too tired to dig," Susan replied.

"Oh no. Was it because I was talking in my sleep — again?" Will asked.

"I wish you were talking. At 3 a.m., you were singing in your sleep!"

Will walked to the refrigerator and removed a half-gallon of orange juice.

"Did I at least sing on key?"

"Nope. You 'sang' 'Oye Como Va.'"

"That's weird," Will said as she yawned and he twisted opened the orange juice. "We've known each other for twenty years and I never talked or even hummed while I slept. Now, that makes that—God, how many nights in a row have I woke you up?"

"You started yapping in your sleep two nights ago, hon," she said.

"Now I'm singing at 3 AM!? Maybe it was something I ate."

"Hmm. Could be. You know, it all started after we went out for Mexican food."

"It did. I—"

Will shivered as if he was just shoved into a closet-sized freezer.

"Th-th-at's weird. I'm f-f-f-reezing. Maybe it really was something in that f-f-f-f-f-ood."

Susan stood and looked closer at his now pale face.

"What's wrong?"

"I-I feel weird... bloated... gassy... Excuse me. This isn't going to sound or smell pretty."

Will stood and lifted his right leg to release gas. His bathrobe moved like a flag getting hit by a violent gust of wind. Then he and Susan heard a male's voice sing.

"Oye como va, toledo. Bien como sa."

Susan laughed and said, "You can throw your voice so it comes out of your ass? Talk about a marketable talent."

"But that voice wasn't mine! Who-who-said that?"

"I'm right behind you, muchacho," the voice answered.

Susan ran behind Will and hopelessly looked for the voice's owner. She lifted his bathrobe only to see his backside.

"Show yourself!" she demanded.

"Put your right hand high in the air, senorita."

Susan obeyed.

"It's in the air. Now what?"

"Slowly lower that muy bonita hand, senorita."

As Susan's hand lowered, the voice said: "You're getting warm... warmer... warmest to me!"

Susan's hand rested and covered Will's butt. A muffled voice then cackled:

"Get your hand off me! Help! Policia! I'm getting muy pawed!"

Susan's palm covered her opened mouth as she gasped. "Honey! Your butt just vibrated when that guy talked! Unless... were you using my vibrator in the privacy of our home and you had an, uh, a sexual misadventure?"

"Of course not!! Just w-w-ho are you in me?" a frightened Will asked.

"A ghost on crack. Perdone. I should say a ghost in your crack."

"What are you doing inside my husband?" Susan asked.

"My name ess Juan Jimenez. In my mortal life, I cooked for Consuelo."

"Is that the same Consuelo who owns 'Consuelo's Restaurante?'" Will asked.

"Where we had that Mexican food two days ago!" Susan added.

"Si. Two years ago, I was Consuelo's secret lover. Well, I was secret until Consuelo's husband caught us canoodling and 'cocaine-ing' in his kitchen. Consuelo's Gringo husband suffocated my pretty face in a pot of refried beans at 3AM. On the anniversary of my murder, my soul rises from the bottom of a pot of refried beans and settles in — a Gringo!"

"You mean — me?" Will said, his voice cracking.

"Si. You ate me one night, now you have me this morning."

"Great. I've got a spirit in my sphincter?"

"Sure do! Just don't ask to move in with me. There's not much space in here... only room for one. And I got this one!"

"Scoot! Vamos already!" Susan ordered, smacking Will hard on his backside.

"Ow! What are you doing?" Will asked.

"I'm just trying to get Juan to find another ass to haunt."

"Tough tamales. I'm staying in your man's can."

"Me amigo, Juan. Isn't this between you and Consuelo?" Will asked.

"Si. So?"

Susan picked up her cellphone and speed dialed "Consuelo's Restaurant."

"Then maybe Consuelo can talk you out of him. Hello? Who am I speaking to?"

"This is Consuelo. May I help you?"

"Yes. My husband has a man in his ass!"

"If that's what he likes, that's what he likes," Consuelo replied.

"No! I mean—oh, you talk to him."

Susan placed the phone flat against Will's butt; only to hear Consuelo say, "May I help you? Hello? Hello? What the hell is this?!"

"Hable, Juan. Por favor? Double por favor?" Will pleaded; only to get back silence.

"Sorry but I'm not in the mood to talk to an asshole —like you!" Consuelo said before she hung up.

Susan left the kitchen and turned on their bathtub's water.

"Now you listen to me, Will," Juan slurred. "The cocaine I took, I feel it's wearing off. So this is what I want you to do. Go and swallow ten pounds of cocaine. That oughta last me a year until I rise up on my next anniversary."

"But if I eat all that blow, it'll kill me."

"Si and so? That's a small price to pay for me getting *real* high! No? Ha ha ho!"

Susan entered the kitchen and motioned for Will to follow her into the bathroom. Will saw the tub of water, nodded and removed his clothes.

"Hey Will. Is this butt cable-ready? Maybe I'll get 'Cine-Ass.'"

Will sat in the filled tub.

"Drown you loco psycho!" Susan exclaimed.

Abruptly, the bath water turned black, wildly bubbled and Juan's voice gurgled.

"Nice try but this ghost is staying! Rent free!"

"That's what *you* think!" Will said. He jumped from the tub, ran to his bedroom and removed the old wooden crucifix that his mother had given him for him confirmation from the wall. The crucifix was at least two feet long.

"Don't put it in! That won't fit, honey!" Susan said.

"I have no choice!" Will said. He bent over, held the crucifix high in the air and barked:

"May the power of Christ compel you to leave already!"

"Look, ass hombre. If you're trying to shove a cross up you, that just won't work, man! Besides, if a cross on a colon isn't a mortal sin… what is?" Juan laughed.

Will threw the crucifix on the floor, ran back to the bathroom, rummaged through the medicine cabinet, and removed a dusty bottle of "Ex-Lax."

"Let the ass-orcism begin!" he announced.

As Will guzzled the bottle, he heard:

"No! Not that!" Juan cried. "No! Stop! Alto! Por favor!"

"Hasta la vista, keister squatter!" Susan said.

"I'm melting away… melting… melting… adios… What a world, what a… Oye como… Ahhhhhhhhhhhhhh —dios!"

"We killed your ass clown! We did it!" Susan exclaimed. They danced and hugged their way back to the kitchen table.

"Whew. Talk about food haunting you!" Will added. "If this doesn't call for a celebration, nothing does!"

"Hmm… How should we celebrate?" she cooed then kissed him.

"We celebrate a killing by killing brain cells! I hereby proclaim this a Mimosa morning!"

"Sorry. It's too early in the morning for me to drink fine French champagne."

"It's never too early for me."

He went to their liquor cabinet, removed a bottle of champagne, popped it open and tilted it into a pint beer mug. After Will added a splash of orange juice to the bubbly, he raised his mug high in the air.

"To a guy's death and this guy's 'rebirth!'" He chugged his Mimosa.

Susan reminded him, "And to digging out our car and visiting your in-laws. Remember?"

"I, huh, 'almost' forgot. Okay. After Mimosa-ing, we'll go and get this latest family obligation over."

After Will polished off the bottle, he and Susan walked outside and found their SUV buried in a snowdrift. Will leaned on his snow shovel and gawked at a six-foot white oval mound with four black tires peeking out from its bottom.

"Staring at snow isn't going to melt it," she laughed.

"Ya think?"

91

As he jammed the shovel by the front of their car, he shivered.

"Whew! It got extra-cold all of a sudden."

Susan looked closer at his now pale face.

"What's wrong?"

"I, I feel weird ... and I — I — really, *really* have to pee."

"Can't you hold it in and do it in our apartment?"

"No! I wish I could but I, I—can't!" he screamed as he unzipped his pants and waddled to the sidewalk. "I have to do it... now!"

As a steady stream of urine poured out and fell on the snow-filled sidewalk, he heard a deep voice with a French accent hiss.

"Bonjour! My nom is Jacques Gabin; a painter in mortal life but now I'm inside you in death."

"He... that guy's voice... just made my dick vibrate!" Will gasped.

"Wait. Are you— in Will's member?" Susan asked.

"Oui. I'm a member of his member. And today must be the anniversary of my drowning in that vat of French champagne."

"Don't tell us," Susan pleaded.

"Yes. He drank me, now he drink in my words whenever he pees."

"No! Someone is throwing a French voice at us!" Susan said.

"Yeah. Whoever it is... show yourself!" Will demanded.

"Oui, pee monsieur."

Will's penis behaved as if it was on auto-pilot; moving and squirting yellow lines in the snow to draw a smiling wavy-haired man, a cigarette in a corner of his mouth underneath a mustache and a beret on his head. As pedestrians approached, stared at the still-urinating Will then stepped over his 'painting,' they heard:

"Hurry! Buy my painting before it melts!" the voice said. "Pablo Picasso had his 'Blue Period; ' now Will Fasso has his 'Yellow Period'... *period.*'"

Will's sobs were interrupted by a police car's siren and a burly policeman who didn't appreciate that Will was relieving himself on a sidewalk in broad daylight and screaming that he couldn't stop. The cop could only shake his head and chuckle.

"Just finish up, buddy. Are you going to conceal that water gun, or do you want an indecent exposure ticket?"

"I can't stop! I really can't!"

"Why not?"

"Ask that French guy!" Susan said, pointing at the yellow-lined portrait on the sidewalk.

The cop closely examined the face and gasped.

"I—I'm pretty sure I know this guy," the cop replied. "Yeah, it's definitely him."

"Who is 'him?'" asked Will.

"This creep named Juan Jimenez. I was the first cop on that crime scene."

"Was he suffocated in a pot of refried beans two years ago?" asked Susan.

"That he was. And I wonder if—"

The cop bent down, placed his head near Will's penis and asked it, "Juan? Are you now 'making believing' you're French?"

"Si! I'm es muy French-o!" Juan cackled. "But believe this. Senor Will ate me one night, he still have me this morning and *every* morning!"

-END

To learn more about the author, Mark Daponte, find his author bio at http://www.grivantepress.com/

SUGAR
By Darla Dimmelle

"Can you come over right now?" Honey asked. She sounded better than she had earlier, when she'd spaced out in Kiddo's room and rambled, sweating and shaking like the devil had gotten into her. She sounded calm, miles away from the frantic *I was so scared, he just kept touching me and I didn't even try to stop him.* It made the knot between Kiddo's shoulders loosen a bit.

"Sure, Honey," he said, already looking for his boots. "Gimme twenty minutes."

"I'm at Burner's house."

Kiddo blinked. "Burner left for Colorado State."

"Yeah, and my mom said his parents are on a Christmas cruise, so," she said.

Kiddo's heart thudded. He cleared his throat, and said, "You broke in." This was not the behavior he expected from square Honey, whose most devious act ever, had been legally signing up for a sugar dating website and not even enjoying it. She wouldn't shoplift from Hot Topic or even smoke pot.

She huffed, like Kiddo was the one being difficult. "*Yes.* Get over here and help me," she snapped and hung up.

Oh fuck, Kiddo thought, toeing on his snow boots and fumbling for his car keys. *Shit, fuck shit, shit fuck.*

Burner's parents lived in a nicer neighborhood than his or Honey's, which was why Burner had left town for college and Kiddo and Honey went to Community. Anyone who'd spent an afternoon after school with Burner knew which potted plant they hid their keys under. They would also know that they kenneled their finicky Pomeranian during vacations and that their security code was 00002. Most importantly, and perhaps unfortunately at this moment, Kiddo thought, everyone knew Mrs. Burner, an abstract expressionist, worked in a big, empty, concrete studio where she liked to splatter paint and then hose the remnants down the drain. Burner had done a presentation on it Freshman year, telling the whole English class about his hero, with pictures and everything.

But Kiddo was sure Honey was just fucking with him. She probably just wanted to steal booze, to kick back and watch some TLC on cable. Honey sometimes pulled the Burner's mail when they were out for $5 a day, so it wasn't *that* weird for her to be there. She probably thought this was real fucking funny. And, honestly, he probably would too once he was sure Honey hadn't done anything too dumb.

He parked a block away, stuffed his cold fingers in

his jacket pockets, and stepped over the snowy curb. Cold air freezing down his throat and lungs, he jogged to the big, boxy, environmentally conscious house, sneaking around to the back to get to the studio.

Honey was waiting for him, chewing on her thumbnail in the doorway, brow crinkled in concentration. Her blonde hair had been braided and pinned close to her head, and the makeup she'd mostly cried and rubbed off was still smudging around her eyes and mouth. She smiled when she saw him, though; her pink-banded braces close to glowing in the dim light of the open studio door. She exhaled. Her breath steamed.

"What the fuck?" he hissed. He looked over her shoulder, where Mr. Redacted was sitting, gagged and tied to a chair, struggling. His scuffed-up leather shoes were just brushing the floor drain. Kiddo looked at Honey again, more violently this time, and repeated, "Literally what the fuck, Honey? Oh my fucking God, what the fuck did you *do?*" Still, he followed her in toward warmth and let her shut and lock the cold out.

Mr. Redacted was sitting uncomfortably, looking on the sadder side of forty and gaunt, although he had a good head of hair. He was wearing old dude date clothes– khakis and a button down—and Kiddo remembered him wearing almost the exact same outfit to Woodshop. His skinny shins and ankles were secured firmly to the legs of the chair, his knobbled wrists behind the back, one final black, plush rope tight around his middle. He had a ring gag in, and the tip of his fat pink tongue lolled out of his mouth, spit drooling down his chin. Besides that, though, he looked fine. He pleaded with Kiddo the second he entered his line of vision, which made no one more comfortable.

"You said you'd help me." Honey only looked a little put out by his lack of enthusiasm.

"I thought you were kidding! We were just joking around to make you feel better after a shitty date. Like, *oh, let's torture porn rape revenge this creep! Sure, that sounds fun!* I didn't think you were serious! You can't just—where did you get all this stuff on such short notice?" he asked, distracted, circling the teacher, taking in how high quality all of Honey's tools were. At least the guy wouldn't be getting any rope burn.

"He brought it," Honey said. "I told him I'd let him tie me up for sex if he showed me how to do it to him first." She shrugged. "He thought it was a good idea. Even took a taxi so his wife wouldn't notice the car was missing."

Kiddo only realized he was staring at her when Honey finally met his eyes to offer him a small, hopeful smile. "So, you," he took a second to process. He swallowed. "You invited him here?"

"Yeah, I texted him; said I was so nervous 'cause I'm a virgin and I'd feel better if he'd come over with some wine and, you know, just help me out with that. He was really nice about it. We even got safe words figured out when I mentioned I wanted him to bring stuff. Mine's 'surprise.'" Mr. Redacted moaned and dribble again. Honey scrunched her mouth up for a second as she watched him and then said, "His doesn't matter."

"Honey." He came to stand next to her again. "You can't do a rape revenge if there's no rape. That's just murder. You're safe. Let's go home. Mr. Redacted won't say anything, and he'll leave you alone forever, right?" and Mr. Redacted nodded his head like it might shake the gag off so he could verbally agree, hummed affirmation coming out of his throat, nonetheless.

"No, he won't," Honey said. "If I don't do something, he's going to stay with me forever."

"He's gonna stay with you forever anyway, if you like, *murder him.*"

"You don't get it," she said, and Kiddo crossed his arms, cocked his hip, and waited. Honey exhaled slowly. "You just don't get it. I'm never gonna be able to shake him if I don't do this. He's gonna be on my mind constantly. Every time I go to the grocery store, every time I walk by my old school—I'm gonna worry I'll bump into him. And then what do I do? Do I call him by his first name? Do I acknowledge how immature I am because I couldn't handle an older man whispering in my ear, promising to tie me to a motel headboard? Do I acknowledge him at all?"

"And what about after I numb myself to this particular shitshow?" she continued, a hand coming up to her mouth, teeth halfway to chewing at her cuticles again, her eyes flickering away from Kiddo to bore into the teacher. "How do I ride on an elevator alone with a man, knowing he might want to put me over his knee? That if he said it aloud, I'd just laugh? That I'd freeze-up if he grabbed me? How do I talk to my professors and feel safe anymore?

How do I talk to anyone?"

"Honey," Kiddo tried to say, but she shook her head.

"I can't feel powerless whenever a man is open about what he wants with me. I need to take power," she said and pointed, "I need to take it from him."

"But he doesn't have power. And if he does, you're the one who gave it to him." Kiddo tried to reason, more for his own sake. At the end of this fiasco, he wanted to be able to say at least he'd tried.

"I know." Honey said. "And I gotta stop doing that. But, like, this isn't moral or righteous. He doesn't deserve this. I'm just selfish like that."

And Kiddo got it. At least he understood being selfish. "When his wife realizes he's gone, the cops are gonna find us through his phone. They're going to hassle us to no end. It'll be a complete nightmare. All that other stuff, worrying about classes and grocery stores and elevators—it's not gonna matter if we're in jail."

"Maybe." She shrugged. "But you don't have to stay."

Kiddo felt a pang of hurt in his chest, his stomach. "You know that's not what I meant."

"Yeah. And you know this isn't about getting caught or not. I've been thinking about this a lot. Since I left you," she said, and then she smiled, a glowing, bright, metallic pink smile. "If you don't wanna stay with me, you don't have to."

Kiddo twitched his lips back at her, unhappy, but a good friend. He would hate to have to write her in prison.

He said, "Ride-or-die."

Mr. Redacted drew their attention again, thumping the legs of his chair against the ground, hawking in his throat.

"Should we take off his gag?" Kiddo asked, moving in closer to inspect the man's blotchy face. His eyes got wider, whiter, the closer Kiddo got.

"I mean, you can take it off if you want, but he's just gonna talk about his wife and kids." Honey walked away toward what must have been Mr. Redacted's bag of tricks.

"Oh," Kiddo said, hand frozen a few inches from the strap. "Yeah, okay. Don't want that," and Mr. Redacted began to cry.

Honey plopped the bag in front of them all to look in. She sighed, toeing at it in her dismay. "I really thought he'd bring more stuff."

"There's some clamps." Kiddo pointed.

"What would we do with those?"

"I dunno." He pulled back, clamps now in hand, eyeing their restrained and gagged man up and down. "We could use 'em on his balls."

Honey's face pinched, nose crinkling as Mr. Redacted shook his head, panting wet through his mouth. "I don't want this to get too sexual. CBT this early seems like we're going about this with the wrong intentions."

"I mean," Kiddo dropped the clamps back into the bag, "Aren't we going to castrate him?"

"I guess we have to." Honey crossed her arms as she thought. "I mean, it's a rape revenge, so we sort of have to.

But I figured we'd do that at the end - just considering the blood loss."

Kiddo nodded. "Okay, so that's our finale. What else do you wanna do?"

Honey bit her lip, watched Mr. Redacted without actually seeing him. "I'm gonna go look around Burner's room. Go ahead and change."

"Uh," Kiddo said.

She pointed at her own floral print tote, which was tucked in the corner next to her drying snow boots. And when Kiddo looked in, he saw the swim shirt and shorts he'd left at Honey's house over the summer, when they'd lazed in her backyard kiddie pool and tried to forget that they were starting college in the fall.

"Oh, jeez, Honey, do you really think this is necessary?" But she was already gone. He was alone but since he wasn't comfortable acknowledging the frantic whining behind him without his friend, he faced away and undressed.

When he finished, he busied himself looking through Honey's bag for whatever else she'd bothered to bring. Her phone was tossed haphazardly next to her red swim team one-piece. Next to that, there was a cheap saucepan and an unopened bag of sugar. She'd shoved a crumpled receipt in with them and, scanning it, he saw she'd bought those from the store before coming, along with a couple of candy bars. He found those in the side pocket.

"Hey, can I have this Snickers?" he asked when

Honey stepped back in.

"Oh, yeah, bro, that's for you."

Kiddo said thanks and tossed her the Butterfinger. "What'd you get?"

"Not much," she said, mouth pulling with frustration. "I tried to stick to Burner's room 'cause he's gone and he probably wouldn't realize if anything was moved, anyway. But unless you wanna smoke some, he took most of his stuff with him."

"He left his weed?"

Honey snorted. "He's in Colorado, dude."

"I can't believe I didn't smoke him out before he left."

She just shrugged, Butterfinger in one hand, a few goodies in the other. She dropped them on the floor and snatched her bag. "You want me to snag it?" she asked.

"Huh?" Kiddo had a mouthful of chocolate.

"The weed."

"We can't smoke his stuff," Kiddo choked. "That is, like, so rude, Honey. That breaks a bunch of bro-codes."

She raised an eyebrow and leaned against the doorframe. The plastic of her candy bar crinkled as she broke into it. "It's gonna be a long night."

Kiddo looked at his friend real hard and then huffed a little. "I'm just not comfortable stealing Burner's weed. It seems wrong."

"I'll text him," Honey said, chewing, already pulling her phone out of her bag.

"Yeah, text him."

"I'm doing it," she said.

Kiddo's eyes widened, and he said, "No, wait!"

"What?" Honey blinked, looking up at him. "I already did it."

"Now, he's gonna know we were *here*."

Honey's eyes were already back on her phone screen. "He just texted back. He said it's fine."

"*Honey.*"

"*Relax.* Burner won't rat us out," she promised. They kept looking at each other for a few more seconds until Honey turned her gaze to the man in the chair. She didn't smile, didn't even try to look friendly as she asked, "You wanna smoke?" Mr. Redacted didn't respond immediately, a deer caught in her headlights.

Kiddo felt his entire being rebel at the question. "What the fuck; why are you asking him?"

Honey shrugged, fiddling with the strap of her tote, saying without irony, "He's about to have a bad time."

"Oh, Jesus Christ!"

Mr. Redacted nodded, almost violently, drool dripping down from his chin to his shirt at the movement. Honey finally grinned. "See, he wants some. I'll go get it." She turned to leave again.

"You gotta be fucking kidding me," Kiddo said, but she was already out of the studio garage. He ran a hand through his hair, which was getting greasy from sweat and he wiped his hand on the back of his shorts. "Making me share with a fucking dead guy."

Mr. Redacted made noise, jerking his head like he

was trying to beckon Kiddo over.

"Oh, shut up. *Shut up.* I know Honey thinks she should have broken it off when she found out who you were, but what the fuck is wrong with you? Trying to take out some barely legal school girl you've seen in uniform more times than not." Kiddo finally met his eye, and he was struck by an urge to lean in and jam his finger into the socket. Instead, he said, "Have some fucking integrity," and he went back to ignoring him until Honey came back.

"What were you two talking about?"

"Nothing. I'll roll."

Honey, in her red swimsuit, tossed the sandwich bag and paper over. She'd left her tote behind, maybe in Burner's room when she'd changed. She stepped up to Mr. Redacted. "I'll take that gag off him when you're done." To the teacher, she said, "You be good when I do, or we'll put this right back on."

"You know, you're breaking genre if you help him like this."

"We already broke genre." Honey waved him off. "So, I grabbed Burner's stapler and his pliers."

"What you wanna do with those?" Kiddo asked, busying his hands.

"You know," Honey shrugged, "Staple. Ply. We're sorta limited on options here."

"You wanna ask him?" Kiddo coughed. "I mean, he could have a preference."

"Yeah," and Honey hesitated before stepping over to him. "You want me to use the stapler or the pliers?" she asked softly, holding them apart so he could incline his heads toward his preferred device. He just shook his head.

"Maybe stapler because he's a teacher." Kiddo offered.

"Ah, man, I was thinking pliers 'cause he taught Woodshop."

"Did you use pliers in Woodshop?"

"Yeah?" Honey didn't sound sure, and Kiddo grinned. Honey's whole face relaxed into a smile at the sight. "Let's do the stapler."

Mr. Redacted made another hacking sound, deep in his throat, gagging on the spit pooling out from his mouth. He, once again, cried, his shoulders shaking violently, and Kiddo felt nothing like the pity he should. He felt more scared for himself and Honey.

"We're the Entitlement Generation," he said aloud, making Honey pause. He met her eye as his lips twitched. He tongued the wrap, pinched the edges, and fished for Burner's red zippo lighter. "We're the first selfish people, aren't we?" He lit up.

"Don't make this weird, dude," she laughed and stapled the lobe of Mr. Redacted's ear to his neck. He screamed, a lot and loudly, guttural in his throat as she moved up to pierce cartilage.

"*Shit.*" Kiddo coughed, taking a drag, leaning over to look. It wasn't even bleeding too much, but the man was thrashing around like he was.

She set the stapler down, but when she moved in to touch Mr. Redacted, he flinched away regardless. "Stay still," she hissed. She made meaningful eyes at Kiddo when the man shied away again.

"Fuck." He stepped behind the chair, trying to get an arm around the man's shoulders while still holding his joint. "Shit, fuck, fucking balls—"

"Here, let me hold that." Honey snatched it from his fingers, holding the bud daintily between her thumb and forefinger, pointing it away from her face. With her free hand, she fumbled with the back of the gag. Almost cheek to cheek with the man, she said, "Don't say anything, or I'll stab you in your face."

The first thing Mr. Redacted did was stretch his jaw out, smacking his lips together. He didn't take his eyes off Honey, not that Kiddo could see that from where he was positioned.

"I like the way you're staring at me," Honey said, gaze unwavering, mouth quirking in a smile. Kiddo let go and came to stand next to her. She didn't really look happy. Kiddo took his joint back. "You look like you hate me. You're so scared of me."

"Hey," Kiddo half-scolded. "Us. He's scared of us."

"Oh, right," Honey laughed, high and soft. Kiddo offered the joint to her, and she took it again. "Open up, Daddy."

Mr. Redacted almost flinched from her hand, eyes wide to the point of bulging. She hesitated, stepping back, a surprised smile flashing before shrugging at him and stretching her arm out. She let him lip the joint from her fingers and then took it back after he dragged. She passed to Kiddo, who fitted his mouth where Mr. Redacted's had been and kissed the joint.

"Please," Mr. Redacted whined to Kiddo in a breath of smoke, his shoulders shaking.

Honey clubbed his ear, going for a slap and overestimating the distance. Mr. Redacted made a pitiful sound, and Honey said, "Shh." Kiddo moved closer to eliminate the middleman and help the teacher puff. Honey flitted back to pick up her stapler.

"I think you should talk to him." Kiddo finally said. Honey sent him a look, her eyes widely exaggerated, mouth a flat line. Kiddo blew smoke into Mr. Redacted's face. "I just think you might regret this, and I want you to be sure."

Honey snatched the joint from him and passed to the teacher. "I am sure."

"Really?" Kiddo laughed a little meanly. He gestured at her, feeding smoke into the older man's mouth. "Because you seem like you're stalling."

The look she leveled at him would have chilled his blood if he hadn't known he'd never be the one in the chair. But, he figured, as he took the blunt back so Honey could gag Mr. Redacted again, there was a fine line between playful and punishable as far as Honey was concerned.

She turned to gaze at her man, her hands on her hips, and Kiddo smoked. There was a sense of accomplishment in her face that made him smile even though she wasn't looking. Especially because she wasn't looking. Slowly, as she considered Mr. Redacted and the work she had been doing, her visible pleasure faded. "The ears are kinda boring," she admitted, her thinking face back on. She crossed her arms, and she finally glanced back at her friend. "Are you okay?" she asked, voice soft for him.

"Huh? Oh, yeah." Kiddo said. "This is easier than I thought it would be. We'll probably be racked with guilt later."

"Oh, for sure," Honey nodded, but Kiddo wasn't sure how serious she was about that. She approached the red-faced and trembling man once more and leaned in to inspect his face.

Faster than anyone could expect, he slammed his forehead against her's, hitting against her nose, making her jump back and yelp. He was panting, seething, and when she, laughing, tried to approach again, he went in for another ineffectual lunge. Honey looked back at Kiddo.

"I'm sorry to ask again," she said.

"Yeah, yeah, no problem," Kiddo said, blunt back in his mouth for safekeeping, moving behind Mr. Redacted again to pull him toward his chest and keep him steady.

"Are you just gonna staple his face down?" Kiddo laughed as she grabbed Mr. Redacted's left eyelid and pulled it up. She had some trouble with the angle, and certainly, Mr. Redacted wasn't interested in sitting still, but she got it to work and then did the other one.

After a minute's pause due to her heavy concentration, she said, "I want his tongue sticking out of his mouth. Hold him - hold him *still*, Kiddo, jeez-oh-weez."

"Don't be a taint, Honey," he snapped back, but

Honey wasn't really listening.

Mr. Redacted, whiny like a big, old dog, was bubbling spit out of his mouth, out of his throat, trying to evade her touch. She tried to get a hold of the muscle, clawing it out with two paint-chipped nails; the stapler brandished in her other hand.

"I don't think you can staple through a tongue," Kiddo said. "It's too wet. Too thick."

"His breath smells like ass," she said, moving away to grab the pliers.

"I mean to be fair," Kiddo said, taking a moment to shake out his shoulders, waving the joint around. "The room probably smells like ass to you."

Honey rolled her eyes. Kiddo back in position, she eased the pliers into Mr. Redacted's mouth, finally gripping his wriggling tongue. He squealed and jerked his head back, which tugged even more at the muscle and must have hurt terribly because he made a weak puppy whine and stopped moving. His mouth was bleeding.

Once Honey had it held and extended and Mr. Redacted had grown still, she gently guided the muscle, forcing him to stretch it out, or risk further damage. With some one-handed maneuvering, she brought the stapler back up, lined up the man's tongue and tried to staple the fat, wet thing to his chin. It didn't go through, but Mr. Redacted still sobbed at the punching sound.

"Shit," Honey hissed through her teeth. She looked at him a second longer, formulating a new plan.

"Any time you like, brah." Kiddo said, still talking

awkwardly around the blunt. "I really love holding this dude's dumb head still."

"Shut up, dickass." and she instead lifted his tongue up, fingering the frenulum. It took a moment, but she pulled his bottom lip over his teeth and under his tongue. "Damn, I wish Burner was here," she said. "I could really use another set of hands."

It took her a few tries to get the right angle, to pierce through his plump, lower lip and clip it to his under-tongue, but she got it. When it did, Mr. Redacted wailed high, higher than he had been, until it all cutoff and he choked on his spit. Honey and Kiddo let him go, let him bend forward as much as he could and catch his breath.

His tongue was stuck out of his mouth, obscene, hanging over the pulled tight skin of his chin. The soft cries he made were tiny, Kiddo watched and smoked, as Honey delighted in the back and forth struggle between Mr. Redacted's tongue and lip.

"Hold tight here," Honey said. "I gotta get something from the kitchen."

"Ah, Honey, no, don't leave me here with this guy again."

"Just a minute, dude," she promised and was off. Kiddo turned away from the man and rolled himself another joint.

"I'd say I'm sorry, bro," he said, his words softer than the sounds coming out of the man's mouth, "But what's the fucking point?" Mr. Redacted didn't hear him.

Honey came back, her footsteps heavy and slow. She

was holding a large pot away from her nylon-covered chest, not wanting to burn herself, Mr. Burner's pot-holders fixed over both hands. Whatever was in the pot was hot, boiling, smelling a mix of sweet and carbon, clearly having been left so long it charred.

"Hold him again," she said, her thin arms struggling with the odd angle and the overfull pan. "Tilt his mouth up for me."

"What is that?" Kiddo asked, peeking in.

"Sugar water," she said and then corrected herself. "Well, I guess it's candy at this point. It got too thick."

Mr. Redacted was moaning, speaking without the ability to form words. He was shaking his head a bit, eyes looking up to the ceiling lights so all Honey and Kiddo could see where the whites of his eyes. Kiddo watched him, watched tears run down his blotchy face, and he opened his mouth to say something.

"The candy's gonna cool off," Honey told him, and then she asked, "Is this too much, do you think?"

Kiddo rubbed at his eyes and he looked back at her. She looked worried, and he knew she'd stop if he asked her to, if he said that was what he wanted.

"Nah, Honey," he said, voice scratchy. He cleared his throat. "It's perfect."

"Good." Honey, relieved, let her mouth spread, pink gums and pink braces over white, white teeth. She was a carnivore. She was the cutest maneater he'd ever seen. He wondered if she'd ever really understand what that meant.

He got behind Mr. Redacted, who had at some

point in their conversation lost control of his bladder, finally giving up that last semblance of situational control and pissing himself. Neither of them mentioned it, the sticky, sweet smell of candy overpowering any acrid stench that might be lingering. Ignoring it seemed like the kindest thing to do.

Kiddo held Mr. Redacted steady, but he wasn't struggling that much anymore. His eyes leaked, his mouth open and ready. Honey hefted the heavy pot up, one knee coming up to press against the man's piss-soaked khakis, over his crotch, and she tipped the sugar water in.

It spilled out slowly, first hitting the side of his mouth, up his cheek, burning his forced open left eye, and the sounds he made were worse than when they'd pierced his tongue. Not too loud, they were hoarse, retching, pitiful coughs torn out of his chest and throat.

Honey tipped the pan straight, re-aimed, and finally got it in his mouth. Kiddo watched his throat work, trying to swallow the burning sugar down, fighting to keep that passage unclogged and failing. He made deep gulping sounds, heavy, to the point that his whole chest convulsed.

Inside of Mr. Redacted, soft, warm sugar candy started to harden, to solidify and block his airway. His feet twisted in their binds, the chair legs thumping on the ground, and Honey pulled back, dribbling sugar down his chin and neck. His face turned from blotched red to purple, his cheeks and eyes bulging as he tried violently to swallow, to suck in one breath. Kiddo let him go and let him thrash, let him asphyxiate. Eyes rolling, sludgy sugar oozing out of his pulled taut mouth, he stopped moving.

Kiddo came to stand next to Honey. She put her head on his shoulder.

"You wanna cut his dick off?" Kiddo asked.

"I think I'm tired," she said. "Can we just bury him?"

"Oh," Kiddo put his arm around her waist. "Yeah, sure."

"He's gonna be heavy," Honey told him.

"Yeah, I know."

"I think we should bury him up the hill," she said. "I'll get the shovels." She pulled away, heading out to raid the Burner's tool shed, but she paused and asked, "Do you think we're gonna get caught?" She didn't look or sound scared.

Kiddo shrugged. "Maybe." It wasn't the point, anyway.

They dug up Burner's old pet cat, remembering where he'd buried it before heading up to school. They put the cold remains in Mr. Redacted's bag and dragged it, and the body, to Kiddo's car, which was pulled around for ease of access.

Honey & Kiddo drove to the mountain path they used to hike during high school and spent a few hours dragging the corpse, walking out into the woods, but not too far. They dug through the layer of snow and then the cold, hard ground. They buried him, put some dirt down, and then they buried the cat on top.

"We just *Gone Girl*'d the shit outta this guy," Kiddo

said, stretching out, staring up at the late, late night sky. Despite the cold air, he had his jacket open, cooling off from the long, physical exertion that was grave digging at Christmastime.

This high up and away from the city, he could see the stars. He thought about how cool that was, to be looking up at the stars at that moment with his friend. Honey was curled up at his side, playing with his fingers. The earth under them was soft from being recently tilled, and the blanket they'd spread over it was cool. He took the last joint out of his pocket and lit up again.

Honey looked at him although he couldn't really make out her expression until he flicked the lighter on. She looked happy with him. "Have you even seen *Gone Girl?*" she teased.

"Nah, man. I've been meaning to get around to it."

"Because this isn't really how you *Gone Girl* someone."

"We did more of an *I Spit on Your Grave* thing, huh?"

"Yeah, but that's a good movie too." She sighed and nestled back down, against his shoulder, into the soft down of his old coat. Her hair smelled like sweat and lavender. He was pretty sure he smelled like bud, but she didn't seem to care.

"Hey," he said, nudging her to get her attention again. "Did you know," he swallowed, clearing his throat. "Did you know that statistically, women rate *I Spit on Your Grave* stars higher than men do? Specifically women over

45 and women between the ages of 18 and 29. Like, even though there are moments where it's basically just gang rape porn and the feminist politics are so wack, ladies still," he dragged, "They still really like it. More than men. I just think that's really interesting."

Honey was already laughing before he stopped, but he didn't really notice it until he'd finished. "Oh, yeah? And where'd you learn that, Mr. Philosopher?"

"IMDB."

"Oh, yeah?"

Kiddo laughed too. "Yeah."

"Hey," she pushed up, pulling him up as well. "Teach me how to smoke," she said.

"But you hate smoking? It makes you paranoid."

"I don't think I'll be paranoid. Not with you here." And when Kiddo hesitated, she said, "Come on, dude. Let's get high and go back to Burner's house. We'll rent *Gone Girl* on their Amazon account."

"Okay, okay," he said. She took the blunt from him and he said, "Go ahead and drag. Take a puff and - hold it. Keep holding it. Hold it a bit more and - yeah, go ahead." She exhaled, the smoke wafting up and silver, cradling her cheeks. He smiled, and she smiled. He lay back down and let her puff again.

Passing it back over, she got real close, touched his shoulder, got his attention one last time before she breathed it out. "Spring Break Forever, Kiddo."

Kiddo choked on smoke and laughed and laughed and laughed on top of a dead man.

-END

To learn more about the author, Darla Dimmelle,
find her author bio at http://www.grivantepress.com/

THE HENRY PROBLEM
By John Grey

"Do you love me?" asked Dawn of the man lying naked beside her.

"If I didn't love you, would I have allowed you to eat a chocolate-covered cherry off my navel," replied Byron.

She had to think about it, something she rarely did before or after fruit-enabled sex.

"I did only agree to a regular cherry. I said nothing about chocolate, you naughty boy. I have to watch my figure."

"And such a lovely figure it is. Your breasts are like cantaloupes. Your nipples like blackberries."

"Those were blueberries you were sucking on, you silly man."

"So that's why my lips are stained."

The bedroom window rattled. The curtain billowed. A thundering howl shook the walls of the room.

"Wha… wha… what's that?" asked Byron.

"Oh, it's just my husband."

"Your husband? You told me he was dead."

"I warned you he was dead. There's a difference."

"What does he want?"

"What does any husband want? To make my life as miserable as possible. Dead or alive, it's all the same to him."

"What's he going to do?"

"What can he do? Shake windows. Billow curtains. And howl. Oh, and that."

She pointed toward the end of the bed where the apparition of a middle-aged man suddenly appeared out of the ether. He was adorned, as usual, in his favorite flannel shirt, dungarees and cap.

"Oh, I'm sorry," said the ghost. "I didn't realize there was a dress code."

"I must be seeing things," blurted Byron.

"Of course you are," said the ghost. "That's all the fun of being with a naked person."

"Henry, will you leave us alone," said Dawn.

"You know, I'm very disappointed. When a husband bursts in on his wife and her lover, there should be some kind of panic involved."

"I'm panicking," said Byron.

"But she's not. And you know why she's not. She's done this sort of thing before. Oh, don't think you're the first. By the way, what's that red stain on your navel? It looks like cherry. Do you want me to tell you the story of her and the gardener? Big brute of a man. Dumb as a pitchfork. Knew his fertilizers though. Had a mango fetish from what I remember."

"Can you blame me for having a little melon on the side? The last two years of our marriage were no picnic, Henry," snarled Dawn.

"We were only married two years."

"Don't remind me."

"And those two years were hell."

"Think of it as a sneak preview of your afterlife."

"Well, I'm not in hell if you must know. I'm here. I have unfinished business."

"Then go ahead and finish it."

"I don't appreciate the way my life ended."

"I did," said Dawn.

"You poisoned me," Henry declared.

"You did?" stammered a stunned Byron.

"Of course, I didn't. It was all in the old fool's imagination."

"What about all that weed killer in the shed?"

"The gardener bought it. To kill weeds."

Henry howled even louder. Byron froze with fear. Dawn merely shrugged it off.

"Is that the best you can do? You wailed louder than that when you were alive."

"So did you, my love. Like when you and the plumber thought you had the house to yourself."

"You and the plumber!" blurted out Byron in disgust.

"Sure. Why not? He was a handsome devil. And strong. While he was licking guava juice off my thighs, I ate apples off his ribs."

"That's disgusting," said Byron.

"Granny Smith's. Very juicy as I remember."

"You didn't eat apples off my ribs," said Henry. "Not even on our honeymoon."

"There was a drought that year, if you remember. The orchards failed."

The ghost let out an even louder howl.

"You know, Henry, that can get very annoying," said Dawn.

"That's the general idea. I intend to make your life a misery from now until doomsday. And beyond."

"We'll see about that."

"Nothing you can do about it. You can't kill me a second time."

"I didn't kill you the first time."

As Henry and Dawn carried on their conversation, Byron's demeanor changed from one of total shock to an overwhelming desire to extricate himself from the situation. While he liked Dawn, there were other grapes on his particular vine who weren't haunted by the ghost of their dead husband. He rose from the bed and reached down for his clothes.

"Leaving so soon," said Henry. "You're gonna miss the best part."

With that, Henry's head suddenly floated away from his neck and placed itself front and center in Dawn's face.

"Is that the best you can do," she said.

He then rejoined the rest of himself and spread his body thin and wide over the bed like a mosquito net. Dawn poked her finger right through the ghost.

"There never was much to you, Henry."

Byron dressed himself in a stumbling, anxious fashion. Dawn lay on her back as she took in Henry's antics.

"Let's face it, Henry," she said. "There's nothing you can do to screw up my life."

"Is that so? Then look at your boyfriend. Apparently, he's not into threesomes. Don't worry young man. There's plenty of fruit to go around."

But Byron didn't hear Henry's last words. His disheveled figure had already made his way quickly down the stairs and out the door.

"Aha!" said Henry. "Alone at last."

The next night, Dawn could hear the van coming long before it entered the dead-end street on which her large Victorian house stood. The exhaust sounded like an elephant with strep throat. She peered out the bedroom window for a view of its approach. Unfortunately, the smoke pouring out of the engine enveloped the vehicle.

But, once it came to an ear-popping stop and its two occupants emerged, the smoke had cleared enough for Dawn to observe the wreck on wheels that had shaken the foundations of every dwelling in the neighborhood. The older of the duo was a figure as decrepit as his van. He limped up the path toward her door while the other, who appeared to be no more than a boy, was struggling to unlatch the back of the vehicle.

"Colin Cooper, at your service," the visitor announced

as Dawn opened the door.

"Mister Cooper, come on in."

As the disheveled figure made his way into the foyer, he turned to call out to the boy who was struggling with a large box that was half-in, half-out of the van.

"Don't take all day with that, Mason!" he cried out.

As more and more of the box tipped over the edge of the vehicle's doorway, it threatened to topple on top of the boy.

"He's such a useless piece of crap," said Colin to Dawn, as he surveyed the interior of her ground floor. "Nice house. Victorian, huh? Ghosts love this kinda stuff."

He then shifted his attention to his helper. "Get with the program, Mason!"

The boy fell to the ground under the weight of the box. It thumped into his prone chest.

"Should we help him?" asked Dawn.

"No, no. The kid's gotta learn a lesson if he wants to be like his old man. Nothing comes easy in life. I should know. I didn't get to be who I am today by lying around on the sidewalk. You don't happen to have a spittoon, do you? No, I suppose not. I just thought this house being so old, you might... never mind. I'd like to tell you that the boy takes after his mother but she's doing time for armed robbery, so that don't work. Nah, he's nothing like Deadeye Dora. Anyhow, to business. From what you said on the phone, you want me to get rid of your husband."

"Yes."

"Which brings me to the question I like to get out of the way up-front. Is your husband actually dead?"

"Well, of course, he's dead."

"I just gotta ask, that's all. Had a case this past month. She said her husband was an evil spirit. And she wanted to be rid of him forever. Turns out he wasn't even dead. Just sleeping it off upstairs. That's not what I do, you understand. So I gave her the name and number of this guy I know."

"My husband is dead all right."

"That's good. That's good."

"I used to think so," Dawn sighed.

"I don't want to have to haul all my stuff in here if it ain't gonna be needed. Violent death was it?"

"Heart attack."

Colin thought about that for a moment.

"Interesting. Most heart attack victims, at least in my experience, don't return from the other side to do their usual mischief. You didn't frighten him to death, did you?"

"Of course not. He thought I was trying to poison him."

"And were you?"

"No. Well, maybe a drop here and there. But he was fanatical about it. It got so he wouldn't eat hardly anything I cooked for him. He just seemed to waste away. Unfortunately, he didn't waste away enough. And now I can't get rid of him. You know, if he hadn't been rich, I never would have married the guy."

The sorry looking figure of Mason finally made it to the front door, dragging Colin's box of tricks behind him. With great effort, he managed to maneuver it over the threshold and into the foyer. The red-faced boy was on the verge of collapse.

"Lazy good for nothing," Colin snarled. "We can't keep this nice lady waiting. She wants to get rid of her husband."

Mason tried to apologize but didn't have the strength.

"He was supposed to take over the business. Little chance of that. Once I'm gone, all those restless spirits can rest easy. This piece of doo-doo won't be bothering them."

Dawn risked a peek inside Colin's mishmash of apparatus. The items that caught her attention were a piece of equipment that looked like a hookah, some bottles of liquid labelled with X's and what appeared to be a detachable clerical collar.

"Ah that," said Colin, noting her interest. "I don't think that'll be needed in your case. You haven't broken out in large red spots, have you? You're not spitting up green bile?" Dawn shook her head. "That's strictly for exorcisms. Not much of a call for them anymore. I'd like to do one on this kid of mine, though."

Mason stepped back from his father.

"Now all we need do now is sign the contract," he continued.

She ushered him into the kitchen where he presented her with a coffee-stained piece of paper.

"Why does it say Mangini's Exterminators at the top?"

"It's from my old job. Don't worry about that. Mangini went bankrupt. I managed to grab some of his stationery before his furniture was repossessed."

Once the signing was completed, the trio then decamped to Dawn's bedroom. Here, the hookah took pride of place.

"So this is where he shows up," said Colin. "The bedroom. I'm not surprised. You know something, sex is what husbands miss most once they're dead. Even when they're alive, some of them. They're naturally drawn to the place where they last got to buck the beaver. Excuse my language. Don't you tell your mother I said that, Mason. Now why don't you get ready for bed, the missus and I'll get this here contraption started."

"What does it do?"

"It emits this special concoction. The formula is known to myself and very few others. It goes back to the Rose Temples. Have you ever heard of them?"

"No."

"They were a secret society run by the Pope. A long long time ago. Don't worry. This stuff is harmless to the living. But the dead can't stand it. It's like pissing on your garden to keep the rabbits away. Don't you repeat that, Mason."

Dawn retreated to the bathroom with the least revealing of all her sleepwear. By the time she reemerged, the Hookah-like instrument was wafting a blue smoke to various parts of the room. Once Dawn got a whiff of it, she coughed violently.

"Are you sure this stuff is okay?"

"Missus, I've been working with this formula for twelve months. And look at me. I'm in perfect health. Believe me, the Rose Temples knew what they were doing. They had their own secret handshakes. Just like the Masons. Not like you, Mason."

Dawn wasn't all that convinced, but she crawled under the blankets, pulled them up to her chin, turned out the light, rolled over and pretended to be asleep.

"I'm scared," whispered Mason to his father.

"How many times have I told you, stupid," he whispered in return. "There's no such thing as ghosts."

"But you're a ghostbuster."

"And so I will be until the pillow factory starts hiring."

"And this lady…"

"Keep quiet. You want to eat, don't you? If only Dora had let me know where she stashed the loot, I wouldn't have to do this shit. Don't tell your mother I said that."

More and more blue smoke poured out of the hookah. Colin didn't immediately notice that some of the stuff was coalescing into a face, a body, a distinctive human shape. It was Mason who first glimpsed it.

"What's that, Dad?"

"That's Henry," explained Dawn.

"Henry?" was Colin's response. "Henry who?"

"My husband. The dead guy you're supposed to send packing."

Colin took a second look at the figure emerging from the mist. And then a third. When it came to a fourth time, his nerves decided that was enough looking. He grabbed his son by the nape of the neck and made it out of that bedroom, down the stairs and through the front door in a time that would have won gold at the Olympics were the sprint-with-squealing-child-in-tow an event.

"Really Dawn, the company you keep," said Harry once

the hubbub had died down.

"I lived with you for two years. Anything has to be better."

"What's with all this smoke."

"I was having the place fumigated. I have a pest I want to get rid of."

"If you're referring to me, then you'll have to do better. Sadly, my sense of smell got left behind when I died but, from the looks of this stuff, I'd say you won't have to worry about roaches for the next two years."

"Will you just leave me alone?"

Dawn rolled over, made an attempt to sleep.

"You know if you hadn't poisoned me, none of this would be happening. I'd still be alive."

"And maybe I would've taken poison myself."

"That's no way to talk. You have all your life ahead of you."

"And the last thing I want is to have all your life ahead of me as well."

Though Byron and his chocolate-covered cherries never did return, Dawn was soon dating again. And, though Ted wasn't the handsomest man in town, he had something that other guys didn't. He was proprietor of his own retail fruit business. Now there would be no limit to Dawn's passions. Here was a man who could get his masculine hands on a melon, a cumquat or a ripe, succulent pear at a moment's notice. And he had many a body part that would make such delicious fruits most welcome. She looked forward to a lifetime of sweat-flavored juice from the sweet to the tart trickling down her chin.

Ted had a dwelling of his own but he'd installed his aging parents within its cozy dimensions. Bringing a woman home with him for more than a slice of peach pie was out of the question. Only Dawn's old Victorian manor offered the kind of seclusion where plums and apricots could be consumed within the safety of each other's flesh. But there was Henry to contend with. He had already scared away one inamorato as well as having put the town's only ghost busting firm out of business. There was no way she could sell the place, not with Henry installed and, no doubt, eager to chase away any prospective buyers. And she was not in a secure enough place financially to just pack up and leave.

"You really are an asshole, Henry," was her typical greeting when he made his nightly appearance.

"But I'm not a poisoner."

"You know I really wish I had poisoned you. It would have given me so much pleasure."

"Speaking of pleasure. Are you getting any, my dear?"

If Dawn had access to a persimmon at that very moment, she would have tossed it through his face.

Dawn's relationship with Ted didn't really blossom until she finally got around to tossing out the stuff that the Coopers had left behind in their sudden, unexpected exit. She had held onto it for a few weeks in anticipation they would return for the junk. But that no longer appeared to be the case.

She poured all the liquids down the sink. From down below, somewhere in the pipes, she could distinctly make out the death-throes of innumerable insects. She left the hookah out on the sidewalk. It only lasted as long as the next passing group of high school students.

She was almost at the bottom of the box that Mason had painfully hauled into her house when she came upon a couple of items that would change her life forever. One was the snap-on priest's collar. The second was a dusty old book titled "Exorcism For Dummies."

Dawn never once believed the ritual would actually work. Nor did Henry.

"An exorcism. You've got to be joking. I'm not possessed."

"This house is."

"It's all a lot of meaningless crap."

But Dawn didn't listen to him. She continued to sprout the text in the book and Henry's expression slowly changed from a smirk to one of unease, especially when his precious ghostly legs and arms began to fade.

"This is not something you should mess with," he protested.

"You are something I never should have messed with."

"Poisoner," he snarled as his face suddenly completed the vanishing by melting into thin air.

Dawn snapped the book shut in triumph. Henry never reappeared. But, in the days to come, that fruit truck showed up at her front door on a more than regular basis.

-END

To learn more about the author, John Grey,
find his author bio at http://www.grivantepress.com/

NIBBLE, NIBBLE, MY WOLF
By J.L. Boekestein

No, I don't have a house you can eat. You have it all wrong.

Imagine, a gingerbread house you can just sink your teeth in. That would not work, would it now? The birds and the beasts would be nibbling all day and before you know it, I would be homeless.

You can't eat my house, sweetheart.
But you can eat me.

There were four of them, naked, rock hard cocks, horny as starved demons. Lean bodies, some with scars. Fighting men's bodies.

She liked that.

Oh, that had been their plans when they arrived. Four dangerous men and one woman alone? They had been joking and jockeying. Who first? What to do? How many times? Would she beg? Would she cry?

They had grinned when they saw her.

Pretty fuckmeat.

She had smiled, a coy fox-like smile, when she saw them.

Nice fuckbodies.

Then they smelled her delicious body.

"Come inside, and get out off those clothes," she had ordered. They had no choice.

The four naked men moved around in the twilight of the hovel. A dying fire and one oil lamp were the only sources of light, just enough to see her beautiful body, her golden hair.

She was standing, naked beside the fireplace. "Taste my skin," she ordered. "Gently."

Four men, horny and hot, wanting to fuck and pound and ravish her. Their lips tasted her skin, something in between kissing, sucking and licking. One nibbled on her neck, one covered her breasts with his lips, one worshiped her buttocks, one served her thighs and her womanhood.

She tasted delicious. A bit like gingerbread.

Four men. It had been a while, and she never had four men at the same time. Two a few times, yes. But four... She grinned evilly. The things she would do!

"You... You can use your hands too."

They did. Four mouths, eight hands, forty fingers. Strong hands, used to wielding weapons. Kneading, touching, caressing, stroking, softly pinching everywhere.

Tenderizing her.

One kissed her hands, took her fingers in his mouth, his tongue tickling against her flesh.

Another spread her buttocks, his mouth making his way down between that valley of flesh, to finally rest and linger at the well near the end of the ravine.

Her eyes flew open. Now that was something she had not felt before! That definitely was a keeper!

"Go on."

Hands cupping her breasts, fingertips massaging her nipples. *Nice.*

A hard cock, stroking against her thigh, by accident. She took it in her hand. Warm and big and hard.

She was going to enjoy this so much! Four hard men, bad men, angry men. She would play with them, let them please her, make their teeth grind and their anger flare. They would fuck her all night long until she had enough, and then some more. They wanted to fuck her! Well, she would fuck *them.*

But first, she had to seal her control over them. Her fragrance was one thing, but in the heat of sex, that sometimes wasn't enough. There had been that one time with that guy who had his nose buried in her intimate parts and... Now, *that* had been embarrassing.

No, they had to taste her, to *eat* her. Only with her inside them, her control would be total. At least for a few days.

Long enough.

"Kneel in front of me."

They knelt, all four of them. Her love slaves.

It was good to be a witch.

Of course, magic had its price. Power always had a price.

Which part?

It would hurt. It always did.

Her body would recover, leaving no trace as usual. Regrowing what was lost in a few hours.

But it *would* hurt.

Fingers. It was by far the easiest and less painful option. Two of each hand. *Damn, that is what you get with four men. But it will be worth it.*

She started with the man on her left. He was the oldest of the four, their captain. A veteran who had killed over a dozen men, most of them in battle. She offered him the ring finger of her left hand. His lips closed around her flesh.

With her big blue eyes, she looked into his own. She swallowed before she spoke: "Bite it off and eat it. Chew it, taste it, swallow all of it."

His yellow teeth dug into her flesh.

The pain was excruciating. So. Bad.

His molars had caught her finger, his incisors were sawing through skin and flesh and tendons.

Dizzily she pulled back her hand, minus one finger. She did not bleed.

He kept watching her while he chewed on her flesh.

It tasted sweet and spicy. Gingerbread like.

He swallowed. He was not happy, wanted to throw

up probably, but didn't.

He was hers, from top to toe, mind and body, his soul. All, for a few days.

With bone white cheeks she offered the middle finger of her left hand to the next man. "Bite it off and eat it." *One down, three to go.*

The pain was worse every time.

Finally, she was done. She sat on the bed, feeling both her hands throb. The four men were still kneeling, all watching her.

Damnation, next time I try something else. How much would my little toe hurt?

That was next time. Now she wanted what she paid for.

She looked at the four men. They were excited. *She* was excited. The hot, heady smell of anticipation filled the air.

"And now fuck me."

When the morning broke, the five of them were in bed. One man on each side, two of them at her feet.

She yawned like a satisfied cat. That had been... Wow!

Her hand had healed, all her fingers were back. It had been *so* worth it.

"Tell me," she said to the captain, "Where are you from and why did you come here?" It did not interest her, but she wanted to be distracted, savor their touch and warmth for a little while longer, before she disposed of them. They *had* meant to rape and kill her.

The captain's story was not that long. He told her about their mission, he told her who paid their coin.

Now, that did surprise her. Oh, the anger she felt!

Old wounds, they run deep.

Old hates never die.

She ordered the men to dress and take their gear and weapons.

"Return to her," she said. "Tell her you want a private audience, to make your report. She will, she trusts you. If you are alone with her, grab her. Pull back her beautiful head and cut her throat. But before you do that, when you four are holding her, when one of you pulls her hair and when another one has his knife against her throat, when she is too afraid to scream, when her eyes can only beg, then whisper in her ear that this is the revenge of her own, true daughter that she left behind in the woods so long ago. Before she married into wealth and status.

"After she is dead, kill yourselves. Do you understand?"

The four men nodded, completely under her spell.

"Be gone."

Ready for danger Hansen entered the glade in the heart of the woods. There was a well, a moss covered hovel, a little garden, some chickens. Nothing special.

He was a woodsman, a huntsman, strong but weary. The last few days he had been on the run for the Queen's guards. He lied to her Highness about killing her stepdaughter - she had such lovely white skin. Or was it about that other girl in the woods, the one with the red hood? Rumors and acquisitions flew, but the only fact was that he was on the run.

And now he was here.

In the doorway of the hovel appeared a woman. Long yellow hair, a blue dress with a white apron. She had a fox-like smile on her face and big eyes of the deepest blue the huntsman had ever seen.

A subtle smell seemed to linger in the air. Something... Something sensuous.

"A good day to you, ma'am," Hansen said. He was a woodsman, but he had been at court.

"The same to you," the woman replied. "My name is Gretchen. Do you seek shelter?"

He hesitated. He needed shelter, but did he want it?

"No offense, ma'am, but they say you are a witch."

Gretchen shrugged. "People say a lot of things. They say you took the Queen's stepdaughter with you in the woods and cut out her heart. Would you believe that?"

How does she know?

He looked at the young woman who clearly was a witch. "Do you believe I did?"

Again she shrugged. "The Queen's men are after you, huntsman. I promise you they will not find you while you are here. *I* decide who is welcome and who is not."

He desperately needed a place to stay. A hot meal, a safe night's sleep.

She is a pretty thing, she is. That smell, it kept teasing him. First, he could not place it. Sweet like mead, hearty like pork, intoxicating like wine.

It is her, he realized. The smell belonged to her. It made his heart beat quicker, and he felt the spark of a fire, down there.

Without noticing himself, he licked his lips. "I seek shelter, and if I am welcome, I would like to stay the night."

There was an unspoken question in his words. Welcome to what?

"You are welcome. Come inside."

Did she mean...? Maybe, maybe not.

"Thank you, Gretchen. My name is-"

"Hansen, I know."

Witch, witch, witch. Still, he did not have much choice. And now he was two steps closer she smelled even more delicious. He felt his cock turn hard.

What is this, some enchantment?

Hansen followed Gretchen inside. Her ass moved under her skirt, her hips swung, her hair was a golden waterfall, but he kept his hands to himself.

Gretchen looked back and smiled as if she knew what he was thinking.

Maybe she did.

A fireplace, some cupboards of carved out wood, a bed. It wasn't much, but it was clean. Hansen didn't pay much attention. That smell, *her* smell was overwhelming inside the little house.

He... His member was stiff by now and strange

enough he felt his belly rumble. The smell made his mouth water.

What is happening?

He didn't think anymore when she flung her arms around his neck and kissed him.

Oh, she was *very* fine. Lips, hot like embers. A kiss... a kiss fierce like a charging army, fresh like a mountain spring, sweet like honey, hungry like a pack of ravenous wolves. One could easily drown in such a kiss. Yes, one could.

He was Hansen, woodsman, the Queen's former—and by now disgraced and wanted—huntsman. He didn't rise to that position by being weak willed or dim-witted.

No.

He threw her on the bed. He was powerful, he was quick. He surprised her.

Hansen's left hand was around Gretchen's throat. In his other hand, he held his big hunting knife, the tip resting under her left bosom, ready to plunge into her heart.

"What do you want, milady?" he asked coldly. He didn't feel cold. Not at all. He damn well felt like he was on fire. He wanted... He wanted... Oh, he knew perfectly well what *he* wanted.

Gretchen started to wriggle but stopped when his merciless fingers took her breath away and the steel of his knife pierced the fabric of her dress and rested against her skin.

"The same as you," she managed to say, laying perfectly still. She looked at him with those big blue eyes, her fox-smile hadn't left her lips but was a bit less sure right now. "To fuck."

Hansen released his grip a little. Enough for her to take a breath of air.

"*Why* do you want to do that, milady?"

Now Gretchen looked puzzled. "Because I want it. You are here Hansen, you aren't bad looking. It gets lonely here in the woods. Don't you want me?"

For a moment Hansen did not say anything. Finally, he said: "You are a witch. I am afraid if I lay with you, I will end up dead, lose my soul, get enslaved or harmed in any other way. Somehow you knew I was coming, who I am. That smell... You are using some enchantment to snare me. Are you trying to capture me so you can sell me to the Queen's men?"

"I would never do that!" There ran a fire in her eyes. "Nor will I harm you, unless you harm me, Hansen. Either go now, or stay with me for the night so we can enjoy each other. I will not harm you."

"You swear?"

"I swear on the sun and the moon, on all angels and devils, on the saints and sinners, on my life and the lives of the ones I love."

It was a good oath, but not enough for him.

Hansen took his hunting knife and held it up to her face.

She froze, for the first time a flicker of fear was visible in her eyes. Fear and something else.

"Swear it on the knife. Its steel will cut your flesh, its

point will pierce your skin, it will taste your blood if you betray me."

Gretchen licked her lips. After a moment, challenging him with silence, she said: "I swear. On your knife."

"Good. Now kiss the steel to close the deal."

He was a cruel, tricky bastard, Hansen the huntsman. Strong and a little bit nasty. Like a wolf. O, it was as shame she would have to let him go, but she had no choice. He made her promise. And it was for the better. One shouldn't keep a wolf in captivity. Just enjoy its power and wickedness as long as you could.

Gretchen the witch kissed the steel hunting knife of Hansen the huntsman, sealing her promise.

He plunged his knife in the headboard of the bed.

She squealed happily when he took her in his arms.

Giving a man control was *very* different from what she was used too. Somehow his dominance over her, forcing a promise from her lips, had broken the spell of her fragrance. Oh yes, he still was hot and horny, just like all other men, but she could not order him around.

Gretchen was not sure she actually wanted to boss Hansen around. Letting him lead had its advantages.

So far, so good!

She didn't have anything to complain about. He might be a woodsman, he definitely knew how to fuck. She suspected the ladies at the court had something to do with that. Those bored, haughty bitches would have eyed a nice piece of meat like the huntsman. Getting lost during a fox hunt? Invitations to a country lodge while their husband was out of town? A quick dirty fuck in the stables? Could you help me out off these riding boots, dear huntsman?

He was a *very* nice fuck, letting her enjoy, giving her not always what she wanted, but certainly what she needed.

But still, the feeling nagged in the back of her mind. He was a dangerous man, with a bloody big knife. A desperate man, on the run. It would be stupid not to make sure he would not hurt her. She would not be breaking her oath.

"Please take the knife," Gretchen whispered in Hansen's ear when he was on and in her. She scratched his back, she ground her pelvis against his.

He didn't ask why. Hansen pulled the knife from the wood.

Such a big piece of steel. She could not help looking at it.

He kept fucking her, but watched her watching his knife.

"I want you to cut off my toe," she said after a while. "My little toe!" she added quickly.

"Why?" He ground and ground her, distracting her.

Damn, it is so much easier when they are under my spell. "I... I want you to... to eat it."

"Cut off and eat your little toe?"

"Yes..."

Hansen shook his head. "I don't know what witch thing that is, but I won't."

"But I need you to eat me!"

"No."

How can I trust you if I can't control you?

He stuck the knife back in the board.

I can't control him. Maybe not even trust him, Gretchen thought. *How do other women handle that?*

"Take me in your mouth," Hansen whispered. "Please."

Ah! Realization dawned.

Maybe she didn't need any magic after all.

The morning fog was still clinging to the trees when Hansen opened the door of the hovel. Standing in the doorway he took a deep breath: wet trees, earth, a thousand different smells. This was his world, the woods.

Gretchen came from the dark of the hovel and flung her arms around his waist, her head resting against his back. Her smell, that devilish enchanting smell, was weak this morning.

"I have to go," Hansen said. He stroked her hair.

"I know," she said. "But will you come back, one day?" It was a request, not an order. An exquisite weird feeling. But she had promised. *Free wolf, dangerous wolf.* In so many ways he was just like her.

"I don't know. The Queen has no doubt put a prize on my head. Her men will be looking for me."

"Don't worry about the Queen's men, or that bitch herself. I have taken care of that."

She looked up, he looked down in her eyes.

"What do you mean?" Hansen asked.

"There were four of them, they came here the day before you arrived. *They* didn't need to hide and backtrack. They figured you would be coming here and wanted to ambush you."

"What did you do to them?" Hansen wanted to know. She was a witch, dangerous and evil by definition. Unless she was forced to behave, by oath.

Gretchen smiled. "They didn't make me promise anything."

Hansen the huntsman, strong, tricky bastard, sometimes bad, mostly good but with a pinch of evil, that lone wolf, decided he didn't want to know. Instead, he kissed Gretchen the witch of the woods.

"I will be back. But I will bring my knife."

Gretchen grinned. "Please do!"

-END

To learn more about the author, J.L. Boekestein, find her author bio at http://www.grivantepress.com/

THE WRATH OF THE BUTTERY BASTARD-TATERS
By Alex Colvin

I came home to find the apartment lights dimmed and old jazz standards playing over the wireless speakers. Before I'd even kicked my shoes off, my boyfriend came over with a glass of wine. "Happy six months, sweetheart," He said.

My 'thank you' was wordless. I said it through a long, slow kiss that made sure he knew what was on my mind. The same thing must have been on his mind as well because the next thing I knew he had me pinned against a wall and was working my dress off while running his hands all over me. We didn't stay there for long. Well, I stayed pressed against the wall. He spun me around and flattened me against it and then took me from behind while running his nails down my back and spanking me. That way is my absolute favorite. Neither of us lasts very long when he takes me like that.

When we'd finished, he kissed me. "We should start

on dinner while it's hot," he said.

I agreed and fetched the glass of wine Daniel had hastily set down before I'd jumped him.

"I made all your favorites," Daniel said, putting our plates on the table. "Peppercorn steaks in a whiskey sauce, beet salad, grilled asparagus and mashed potatoes."

I went to the table where he'd laid out a perfect candlelit dinner. Everything he said was there, and it looked gorgeous. Oh, wait. No. Something was missing. "Lovely," I gave his hand a squeeze. "Where are the mashed potatoes? I'll bring them out."

"I put them in the oven to keep them warm."

So I opened the oven door and found the bowl. It had a lid on it and was perfectly warm to my touch. I set it on the counter and took the lid off, determined to sneak a finger full of mashed potatoes before setting them on the table. I set the lid down on the counter and peered at the taters.

Oh.

Oh god.

Please no.

I was too horrified to scream. I stood in frozen terror at what lay in the bowl before me. It looked like drywall filler. Could it be what I thought it was? I prayed that it wasn't. I had to ask. "So you made mashed potatoes, sweetie?" I called, trying to sound casual.

"Well, instant mashed potatoes."

I went numb with fear, unable to speak, while Daniel continued, "I only had so much time to prepare everything, and it was the easiest corner to cut. Plus they were on sale! I'd made them with tons of butter and milk, so we probably won't even notice the difference!"

I doubted that.

My childhood revolved around this same prepackaged inedible muck and I hate it passionately. The batch Daniel made seemed no different. It simultaneously looked both chalky and gluey. Daniel must have thought they looked godforsaken too, because he added, "the color is a bit off, but it smells lovely."

I said nothing, determined not to spoil the mood. I was touched at what he'd done and didn't want to shut him down tonight. So I set the gloppy false-potatoes on the table and vowed to ignore them. Daniel and I sat down for dinner and I helped myself to the dinner options that were genuinely delicious, and not simply pretending to be real food.

But the taters were as easy to ignore as a rotting corpse draped over our dinner table. I ate everything on my plate that wasn't touching them. I was almost done with my plate and thought victory was in my grasp, but Daniel was too proud of his efforts to let them die, however much they deserved to. "Here, have some potatoes, love," Daniel said, dropping a scoopful onto my plate with a watery splat.

If you think instant mashed potatoes look disgusting in a bowl, when they share a plate with real food, they look like an abomination that could not be of human creation. Nuzzled between Daniel's peppercorn steak and asparagus, it looked pathetic and undead. As the puke-worthy goo settled onto my plate, it seemed to be begging me to finish it and put it out of its miserable existence, one painful mouthful at a time. I found myself hating it for existing and considered avoiding it and everything they touched on my plate. I was just working up the courage to tell Daniel that I couldn't withstand an encounter with mushy wannabe-potatoes when he put a massive forkful of the sludge in his mouth and smiled. "Mmm," He said.

His smile vanished as he tried to chew the abominable substance and discovered its paradoxical texture that managed to be simultaneously dusty and moist. He gagged, valiantly fighting to chew and managed to swallow the mouthful. "Delicious," he said, almost sounding sincere.

I love Daniel dearly and I decided he couldn't go through this alone. We were partners to the end, and I had to at least try it for him. Out of love, I took a moderate forkful, made peace with God and put it in my mouth.

Oh. It's so—my god…

WHY?

The flakes that had been resistant to the milk and butter lacerated the inside of my mouth while the gooey remainder tried to ooze out from between my lips. The gluey papier-mâché texture started wracking up paper-cuts on the insides of my cheeks and on my tongue. I tried to break down the concrete-like texture and consistency by chewing it, that was a huge mistake. Letting it between my teeth simply made it easier for the substance to glue my jaw shut and froze me in mid-chew. Daniel was watching me like a dog waiting for a biscuit, hoping for approval for all of his efforts. I tried to smile, but I didn't dare move my lips for fear of throwing up. My mouth was frozen in place and my eyes went wide with fear.

Daniel noticed.

"Sweetie, if it's crap, don't eat it," he said (to his credit).

"Nnnnnnnnm," I protested, fighting like a demon to chew or swallow the oozy, flechette-ridden sludge.

Okay, so I have to tell you something about myself that's quite personal: I have a gag reflex on a hair-trigger. I sometimes choke on my toothbrush and putting anything big or gross in my mouth on a full stomach can lead to disaster. I'd already eaten most of my dinner and I was trying to suppress my gag reflex as I choked on the potatoes, still trying to wrench my mouth open. And when I finally did manage to pry my jaws apart, I vomited all over the table and what remained of our dinners.

Daniel was really good about it.

I came back from brushing my teeth and found him heating up a tin of soup on the stove. I came up to him from behind and wrapped my arms around him. He didn't acknowledge me and seemed unusually focused on stirring his soup.

"I love you," I said.

"Yep."

Uncomfortable silence.

I glanced at the bowl of vomitable mashed potatoes

and saw it was empty. Daniel had chucked out the rest of them, but the box they came in was still on the counter. I glanced at it. The box was a sludgy green color and read, "*INSTANT MASHED POTATOES: A PRODUCT OF THE SIBERIAN EXPERIMENTAL FOOD SOCIETY.*"

I read on: "*Enjoy scientifically engineered mashed potatoes designed to be the hardiest crop on the planet and to be perfectly delicious! These potatoes are infused with the DNA of bull sharks, hyenas, wolverines and jellyfish to help them survive in the harshest conditions on the planet. Grab a taste of the future while the FDA approval is pending. Enjoy every delicious bite of scientific achievement!*"

Experimental, huh? Well, it sure was a lousy experiment. Daniel must have bought them at that niche food store he likes so much. He was still stirring his almost certainly mixed soup, and I figured I had to try a new tactic to apologize. I turned him to me and kissed him. When we broke apart, I said, "Well, at least now I can deep throat you since I've got an empty stomach."

"Love, you don't have to-".

"No, lets. This evening doesn't have to be a total waste."

I pulled Daniel into the bedroom and sat him down on the bed. I slipped onto my knees in a single motion and started kissing his chest, working my way down to his hips. I worked my usual magic and had him hard before he'd even managed to take his clothes off. He gasped, he clawed my back, he fell back and begged me not to stop, so I didn't. I ran my nails over his thighs and he finished in my throat with a moan. There, I thought, not such a terrible evening after all.

At least, that's what I thought until I heard the sound of breaking glass coming from the kitchen.

"Did I imagine that?" Daniel asked.

"No, I heard it too. Should we go have a look?"

"Let's."

We slipped from our bed and went to the hall. As soon as I stepped out of the bedroom, I heard something tinkling in the kitchen. I hoped it was just the tap dripping and that nothing weird was going on. And oh, how I was wrong.

You know how I said that instant mashed potatoes were an abomination? Well, I was right. More so than I ever could have guessed. I stopped dead when I saw what was going on in the kitchen. They had come to life and from their behavior, were also disposed towards violence and killing people.

I surmised this because the mashed potatoes had congealed into a humanoid being, perhaps two feet tall. It was gelatinous and stumpy and bits of potatoes would occasionally drip off of it. The buttery bastard-taters had crude mitts for hands and a gaping mouth for a face; it also was determined to make itself more dangerous. The mushy hell-spawn had smashed the beer bottles we'd had under the sink and was embedding the shards in its mouth and mitts so it could have both fangs and claws. Amber chunks of glass littered its jaw in rows, and the longer pieces had been pushed into its paws. It sat on the floor like a hideous doughy toddler and picked through the glass to see if it had missed any of the more especially sharp ones.

It stopped.

The sludgy starch-monster turned and looked at me, although it had no eyes to see with. The toothy mouth broke into a grin, and the buttery beast brought its teeth together with the sound of scraping glass. The gooey abomination stumbled to its feet and charged at Daniel and I, claws out and mouth open, a high-pitched howl escaping from its throat.

Daniel screamed. I didn't even manage that, I just fled. Daniel followed, and we retreated to the bedroom and locked the door. I pulled him back from it and we waited, holding each other.

The overly processed living nightmare stopped at the door. There was silence for a moment. Then came the first scrape.

Then the second.

Then the third, louder this time.

The Satanic side dish was trying to claw and bite through the door.

I turned to Daniel. "Call the police!"

"And tell them what?"

"Anything! Just get us help!"

Daniel stumbled to the bed to grab his phone. I just watched the door and listened to the scrapes against the wood. When all of a sudden, they stopped. Daniel and I looked at each other. Was it giving up? Had it died? Were we safe?

I turned back and looked at the door. It wasn't budging, maybe the self-loathing faux-spuds just decided it couldn't cut through—but then I noticed something. There wasn't any light coming in from under the door anymore. The ungodly spud-sludge was blocking it. Then I saw it and realized why no light was getting through.

The sleazy-starch demon was mashing itself right under the door.

Of course. The monster was instant mashed potatoes. It didn't have to be solid. It could get in cracks or gaps. So it was coming for us all the same. Daniel must have realized it too because he shrieked and pointed at the door. I scanned the room for a weapon. We didn't have much in the bedroom, really. Just our dresser, the bed and a bookshelf.

On the dresser, though, was a can of hairspray. That might work, but only if…

I wheeled around to face Daniel, "Do you still smoke weed?"

"What?" His eyes went wide with my question.

"Daniel! Just tell me the truth! Are you still smoking weed behind my back?"

"Fine! Yes! Why are you asking now?"

"Where's your lighter?"

"Bedside table."

I found it. The gloppy sludge-spawn was almost past the door and was congealing back to its humanoid form only a few feet from Daniel and I. I grabbed the hairspray, preparing to strike. Would it die? Would it just keep charging? Could it even feel pain? I certainly hoped it could and that this would stop it.

"Get ready," I said, holding up the hairspray and lighter.

"Jesus Christ!" Daniel said. "You'll burn the building down!"

"Which is why you'll grab the fire extinguisher once you can get to the door! Go get it, run right back and be ready to put the room out!"

Daniel nodded, eyes wide with fear. The Siberian-farmed parasite had slid into the room and was reassembling on the floor, claws and teeth bared. "GO!" I shouted at Daniel, taking aim.

Daniel tore the door open and ran, leaving me alone with the monster.

The lighter lit, I took aim with my hairspray flamethrower. The slimy reanimated spuds sensed an attack and leaped from the jet of flames onto my dresser. Without hesitation, the oozing monster lunged at me, claws extended and jaws open to eviscerate me with its broken rows of glass teeth.

I don't know how I reacted so fast, but I ducked. The demon-taters missed me by inches and landed on the bed with a splat. I pivoted, hairspray still raised, lighter still lit and shot a wave of fire at the wretched reconstituted spud, catching it as it struggled to its feet. The microwavable mistake was engulfed in flame. It let out a high-pitched scream as its mushy flesh withered under my hairspray inferno, causing it to stumble and collapse on the bedding. Even as the buttery beast succumbed to the fire, it took feeble swipes at me with its jagged talons. Its claws raked the mattress, leaving deep gouges, but it advanced no further. The tormented tubers let out a final gasp and then crumbled from its humanoid form, overcome by the flames.

The bedding was also catching fire, but Daniel came roaring in and aimed the fire extinguisher at the dead monster and the bedroom at large. He didn't stop until the canister was empty.

Can't fault him for enthusiasm.

As the chemical fog settled, we were left standing in a powdery room, in front of a smoldering pile of instant mashed potatoes and glass. The bed was ruined, but we were unscathed.

The lighter and hairspray fell from my hands and Daniel set down the fire extinguisher. We looked at each other amidst the smoldering carnage.

"What do we do now?" Daniel asked.

"Want to sit on the balcony?"

"Wait, what? You want to sit outside after all this?"

"Damn it, Daniel. Come on. We could use a quiet moment, we'll talk about it outside."

We went and sat out on the balcony and held hands. After a while, Daniel said, "I wonder if those potatoes were GMOs."

I didn't glorify that comment with an answer. I mean, they were clearly modified in some way, but I wasn't going to follow up on that one.

Daniel squeezed my hand and looked at me. "From now on, I'll make real mashed taters with dinner."

"Agreed."

-END

To learn more about the author, Alex Colvin, find his author bio at http://www.grivantepress.com/

SAUCE
By Steve Carr

Bart lifted the 150-pound barbell on the rack then sat up on the bench and looked around the gym. For a Friday at midnight, it was surprisingly busy.

He stood up and stretched, flexing his rippling muscles barely hidden beneath his bright red tight sleeveless muscle shirt. As he removed the towel from the bench he had been lying on and draped it around his neck, he wondered if he had caught anyone's eye. He hadn't. He went into the locker room. The aroma of sweat and steam from the sauna and showers delighted his senses. He closed his eyes and inhaled.

At his locker, he removed his clothes.

The young man standing at the next locker unabashedly stared. He had a sleeve of fiery tattoos on one arm.

"Hey, if you don't mind a compliment from another guy, you got a nice bod," he said

"Thanks," Bart said as he flashed a brilliantly white

smile. "I'll take compliments wherever I can get them." Bart followed the trail of flames tattooed from the guy's wrist up to his deltoids, then glanced across to his defined pectoral muscles. The skin on his chest was blistered and red. "What happened to your chest?"

The man put several fingers on his chest and winced. "A cooking class accident," he said. He reached out his hand. "My name's Max."

"Mine's Bart," he said shaking Max's hand. "Cooking class? You learning to be a chef?"

"I'm a saucier," Max said. "You a foodie?"

"Not really. I know practically nothing about cooking. What's a saucier?"

"I'm a chef who prepares sauces," Max said.

"I know even less about making sauces," Bart said. "I'm interested in food but between work and coming to the gym I don't have much time for cooking but I'd like to learn."

"I belong to an exclusive cooking club that might interest you," Max said. "After I shower, I'll get one of my cards for you and hopefully you'll come to one of our club meetings. Just so you know, our meetings are clothing optional."

"Nudity is something I do know something about," Bart said, nonchalantly raising his arms and displaying his melon sized biceps.

Sitting across from Janet, Bart swirled the spoon around in his kelp and blueberry smoothie.

"I'm surprised you called me," she said. "It's been months since I last heard from you or saw you."

"I've been busy," he said. He lifted a spoonful of the smoothie to his lips and licked the cold, pale purple mixture with the tip of his tongue. He put the spoon back in the smoothie. "I was having breakfast this morning and wondering why you and I never took our relationship to the next level."

She raised a stick of celery out of her cherry and celery smoothie and bit into it. The crunching sound reverberated in the small juice bar. "You're too busy having a relationship with yourself to include anyone else," she said.

Bart ran his hand across his chest, feeling the sensation of his shirt against his skin. "That's harsh," he said.

She dipped the celery in the mud-colored smoothie then raised the dripping stick to her mouth. "I didn't say it to be mean but you're obsessed with your own body and with yourself." She took another bite.

He put his lips on the straw and sucked a small amount of his smoothie into his mouth and swallowed. "Maybe you're right," he said. "I've been thinking I should get out more, meet new people. Maybe it would help me be less self-involved."

"Maybe it would," she said. She raised her glass to her mouth and took a drink of the smoothie.

"I've been invited to an exclusive cooking club," he said.

She swirled the celery around in her smoothie. "You don't know anything about cooking. Who invited you?"

"Some guy I met at the gym," he said. "He's a saucier. I talked to him on the phone just before I called you. There's a meeting tonight." He paused then added "he said clothing was optional."

Janet leaned back and crossed her arms across her large breasts. "So it's some sort of kinky nudist thing?"

Bart took another drink of his smoothie. "It sounds pretty harmless, actually."

She uncrossed her arms and leaned forward over the table. "As I said it's been a while since I've heard from you. Why are you telling me this?"

"The cooking club thing is new, and I thought you'd like hearing that I was going to it," Bart said.

"So basically you wanted to meet to talk about you?" She stood up. "You'll never change."

She turned and walked out of the juice bar.

Max opened the door wearing a mesh thong and nothing else. "I'm glad you decided to come," he said to Bart.

"Thanks for inviting me." Bart held out a bottle of Ghiradelli chocolate sauce. "I found this in the back of my cupboard."

Max looked at the label. "It's a good brand, though I usually make my own chocolate sauces. But thanks. Come in and let me introduce you to the others," he said as he closed the door.

Max's apartment was large and the living room and kitchen were an open concept design. The three others were seated on stools at the kitchen island. Tomatoes, a can of tomato paste, parsley and garlic cloves were in the middle of the island.

"You can remove as much of your clothes as you want and just leave them on the bench with everyone else's," Max said.

Bart completely undressed, aware that the others were looking at him. He walked to the island.

"This is Monica, Cherry and Mark," Max said pointing to each of them. "Everyone, this is Bart."

The two women had on only panties and Mark was naked. Cherry and Mark were holding hands. They each said hello, politely, but reservedly.

To Bart, they were attractive enough to look at, but he had expected more. Cherry had a great body but the right side of her face was scarred. It was bright red as if the top layer of skin had been peeled away.

Mark had a line of similar scars down his spine.

"I'm making a simple marinara sauce tonight," Max said. "Make yourself comfortable and have a seat and I'll get started."

He sat down next to Monica.

On the other side of the island, Max chopped the parsley and minced the garlic and tossed them into a food processor with the tomatoes and tomato paste. He added some oregano, salt and pepper and turned on the processor.

Max and the others said very little as he cooked.

Bart found himself staring at the large bright red spots on the inside of Monica's thighs.

Max heated olive oil in a pan then added chopped onion to the oil then poured in the blended tomato sauce and a little white wine. When some of the bubbling sauce splattered on his bare abdomen, he moaned softly.

At the end of the evening after everyone had tasted the sauce they politely said goodnight to each other and got dressed and left.

"I hope you enjoyed yourself," Max said as Bart put on his pants.

"It was different," Bart said. "Thanks for inviting me."

As he left, he took the bottle of chocolate sauce that Max had set on the bench.

That night Bart awoke startled out of a dream he mostly forgot as soon as he opened his eyes. What little he did remember involved him having sex with a woman who looked like Monica, but they were in a vat of bubbling marinara sauce as he pumped his big cock in and out of her. In the darkness of his bedroom, he wrapped his hand around his erect dick and stroked it until he shot a huge load of jizz onto his chest. He closed his eyes and went back to sleep.

"Face it man, you're kind of a jerk," Ty said as he peeled the banana and bit into the white, hard pulp.

Bart flicked a breadcrumb from his suit pants.

"Why?"

"I'm totally straight and even I'd let you fuck me, but you're a borderline narcissist," Ty said as he slid the banana between his lips.

"What makes you think that?" Bart said. He stood up and tossed his empty lunch bag into a trash can.

"Janet called me," Ty said. He bit into the banana and swirled the hunk of fruit around in his mouth before swallowing.

Bart looked up at the bright blue sky. "She's calling my friends about me?"

"I'm her friend too, man." He took another bite of the banana.

"I just mentioned I was going to take a cooking class, and she freaked out," Bart said.

Ty swallowed. "She told me about it. She mentioned something about it being for nudists. Did you go?"

Bart straightened his belt, making sure the buckle was perfectly aligned with his pants zipper. "Yeah, I went, but I didn't get it at all. I was totally nude, and no one paid any attention or tried to touch me. It was really weird. All that happened was the host showed us how to make a marinara sauce."

Ty burst out laughing. "Do you even hear yourself when you talk?"

"Why?"

"I'm sure the others there have seen naked guys before," Ty said.

"Yeah man, but you have to admit it. I'm hot." Bart

looked at his watch. "We better get back to the office."

Ty threw the banana peel into the trash can and draped his arm around Bart's shoulders. "I like a good marinara sauce. You'll have to show me how to make it sometime."

At the grocery store, Bart stood at the vegetable bin examining the tomatoes.

"I have some of those at home already," Monica said as she came up beside him.

"Oh, hey," Bart said a bit surprised. "You planning on making Max's marinara sauce?"

"I wasn't until I saw you standing here," she said. "If you have no dinner plans, I could make some pasta and the sauce and we could get to know each other."

"Sure," he said. "At Max's I didn't think you were the least bit interested in knowing me."

"Your body is intimidating," she said.

"It is? Why?"

"There's not a mark on it," she said.

Bart stood in front of his full-length mirror looking at the line of bright red spots that extended from his pecs to the base of his cock. Having the boiling hot marinara sauce dribbled on him by Monica as she rode up and down on his incredibly hard dick had been a first when it came to sex.

It was also the most explosive ejaculation he had ever experienced.

Having his skin scalded heightened the sensations. During the sex, he didn't have to be concerned with pleasing her. The pleasure she was getting from watching his reaction each time the sauce touched his skin seemed more important than having his big cock inside her. He couldn't hide from her that along with the intense pain, he was in near ecstasy during every moment of it.

Looking at his reflection he tilted the pan of boiling chocolate sauce allowing drops to fall on his limp penis. He screamed out in agony as his cock became fully engorged.

"What if I could tell you the way to have the best sex you've ever had?" Bart asked as he inserted his tongue into his ice cream.

"I'd ask how much would it cost me?" Ty said. He put a popsicle in his mouth and sucked on it.

"It won't cost you a thing," Bart said, running his tongue around the rim of the waffle cone. "We have to keep this between us, though."

Ty inserted the popsicle deep into his mouth then slowly pulled it out. "Who am I going to tell?"

"It's sauce," Bart said, biting into the cone.

"Sauce?" Ty said, holding the saliva covered popsicle to his lips. "You mean ingredients in some sauce?"

"No," Bart said, taking another bite of the cone. "Dropping hot sauce onto your skin."

Ty bit into the Popsicle. He let the piece defrost a little on his tongue before swallowing. "What are you saying?"

Bart shoved the last piece of cone and remaining ice cream into his mouth. He stood up and looked around the park and moved his tie aside and unbuttoned his shirt. Holding the shirt open he displayed the large patch of red, blistered skin on his chest and abdomen extending down to the waistband of his pants.

"God, Bart, your skin is scorched," Ty said, his mouth agape.

"I know," Bart said. "And it gives me the biggest hard on ever."

Max answered the knock on his door wearing a black silk bathrobe.

"Did I catch you at a bad time?" Bart asked.

"It's kind of late," Max said. "I thought after the class I'd never see you here again."

"I want to learn more about sauce," Bart said. "Can I come in?"

Max stepped aside and waved him in. "Sure, but it's just you and me."

Bart walked in. "That's okay. Monica broke things off with me."

Max closed the door. "Yeah, I heard you two were seeing each other. What happened?"

"She said it was getting too intense but frankly for me, it was getting boring," Bart said. "You in the mood to fix a sauce?"

"Not really, but I have some leftover mole sauce I could heat up if you want to try it."

"What's mole sauce?" Bart asked.

"It's a Mexican sauce made with chocolate, chili peppers, onions and garlic," Max said.

"Sounds good. Should I take my clothes off?"

"Only if you want to," Max said.

Max went to the refrigerator and took out a bowl and took a sauce pan that was hanging from a hook above the stove.

Bart removed his clothes and laid them on the bench. When Bart sat down at the island, he watched Max pour the thick brown sauce into the pan and put it on the burner. Max removed his bathrobe then turned to Bart.

"Wow," Max exclaimed. "Are you sure you want to do sauce tonight?"

"Why?" Bart said.

"Your skin is really blistered, Bart. You may be overdoing it."

"I do it when I masturbate," Bart said. He ran his hand over the blisters on his chest. As fluid drained from them he smiled. "This will be my first time doing sauce with another guy."

"It can get pretty intense," Max said.

"Let's do it."

"I've stopped going to the gym," Bart said as he bit into one end of the submarine sandwich.

Ty slid a large pickle across his lips. "Why? I thought you lived to work out."

"I've found other ways to appreciate my body," Bart

said.

"I hope you're not talking about that sauce thing again," Ty said.

"In fact I am," Bart said. "You're my best friend, so I have to show you."

Ty licked the juice from the pickle. "What do you mean show me?"

Bart grabbed Ty's pickle and tossed it into the wastebasket. "Follow me." He left his desk and headed toward the men's restroom, followed by Ty.

Standing in a stall and facing the toilet, Bart lowered his pants and underwear and bent over and spread his cheeks.

Ty gasped.

"Beautiful isn't it?" Bart said looking over his shoulder at Ty's horrified gasp.

"What have you been doing to your ass?" Ty asked. "It's burned raw."

"I've been letting another guy sauce me back there," Bart said, smiling.

"I must be an idiot for coming here," Janet said as she entered Bart's apartment.

"I'm glad you did," Bart said. "I was hoping I could show you I can be a much less selfish lover."

"Bart, it wasn't just the sex," she began. "Somehow you have gotten through life without learning how to think about anyone else but yourself."

"I've changed," he said. "Come into the kitchen

while I finish making the sauce for our dinner."

In the kitchen, as Janet bent over the pan of oil and melted butter with white wine, Bart hit her over the head, knocking her out.

When she awoke she was naked and tied spread eagle on his bed. Bart was standing beside the bed, also naked. He was holding the pan of bubbling mixture in his hand.

"Bart, let me up," Janet yelled as she struggled against the ropes around her wrists and ankles.

"I want to show you I can care for you like I care for myself," Bart said, crawling onto the bed between her legs.

"This is rape," Janet screamed at him. "I'll have you put in jail for life."

"I'm not going to rape you, Janet," he said.

Janet stared at the sloughing skin over most of his body below his neck. "Bart, something is wrong with you, with your body. You need help."

"Quiet now, Janet," he said. "You're going to enjoy this just like I do."

Beginning with her eyes, he poured the sauce down her body. As he watched her writhe in pain, he poured the last of it over his face.

He shot a load of his own sauce without even touching his raging hard cock.

-END

To learn more about the author, Steve Carr, find his author bio at http://www.grivantepress.com/

THE CARE AND FEEDING OF YOUR PERSONAL DEMON

By Maxine Kollar

"Shaddafocup," quietly in the hallway.

"Shaddafocup," a little louder in my doorway.

"Shaddafocup!" loudly in my room.

"Daniel Javier Freeman, you better watch your mouth!" seeped in under my door.

My words were screamed through clenched teeth at my mother, who I really do love, and those same words pierced through countless layers of earth and caused a piece of Hell to appear in my room.

Let me catch you up. There is a cauldron of demons in the center of the Earth. All these demons have names. If you call one of their names three times, think Bloody Mary, that demon will fly out of Hell and come to you. I know; I didn't believe it either until I got the name right.

If you're the right type of person, you're going to lose some skin on the quick drag down to Hell but if you're just an average screw-up, then the demon has to bide his time. Sometimes these demons are really good at housework and baking. It doesn't bother them to make scones and vacuum in high heels and pearls to pass the time. However, some of them get rather testy and would rather boil in the oils of Hell than hang out and get involved in whatever boring junk you're up to.

I wanted nothing more than to not see what I was looking at but there he was, looking pissed already. He sniffed me and got really mad because he said I was too innocent to drag back to Hell. The other demons would tease him.

I inexplicably squared my shoulders and retorted that I wasn't all that innocent. I had to wonder whose side I was on. What happened next, trust me, was even stranger.

The damned demon pulled out a pair of horned rimmed glasses and somehow put them on his misshapen face. A whiteboard of sorts appeared in mid-air and the demon's index finger extended to an upsetting length so that it could be used as a pointer.

On the white board, the outlines of two screaming humans appeared. They were surrounded by pulsing waves of color that seemed to be tormenting them. The demon explained that all humans are encircled by their own unique 'moral aura', if you will. Some psychics and all frauds were able to see these auras but since humans are as dumb as shit, they can't figure out what demons and animals have known forever; you can also smell and taste these auras. He then pointed to the first figure. The first piece of filth, he went on, was nice and fair and humble and his aura tastes like lint. The other figure, well this guy was an eleven on the ARS (Asshole Richter Scale) and his aura was delicious.

He then took off the glasses and said to the figures, "Thank you, Mason and Preston. You may return to Hell." The figures nodded and burst into flames as the board faded.

After the demon's finger withdrew to its regular size, he came very close to my face and growled that he was certain, beyond a doubt, (his nostrils filling and flaring for emphasis) that I was too innocent to take back. However, there were some alternatives he was willing to explore with me.

If I asked nicely, he could drag my mother down to Hell and feast on her intestines until the end of all times. You know, while she screamed in the pain of knowing her fate and knowing who had caused it. Of course, doing that to a loved one would mess up my soul so badly that I would follow them down yonder. This is what was called a twofer, and those garnered so many high-fives from the other demons. I thought about the laundry and the pastries and declined.

The next option was not much better. Turns out that if I die by my own hand or in any act of violence while linked with him, he could take me to the Core. He ran off a quick list of effective ways to off myself but ended with suggesting I suffocate myself by sticking my head up my ass or maybe diving into the pile of laundry behind my door. He kicked a stiff sock up into my face for emphasis and I felt my face flush red as I grabbed a pair of dingy underwear off my desk. I didn't love the death option either.

I told him I know plenty of characters that would smell great to him. He looked disgusted, quite a feat, and tells me there are rules he has to abide by. He would gladly take one of those Core-worthy characters but in order to transfer ownership, he takes a moment to bemoan the bureaucratic bullshit of it all, I had to get aforementioned ass-wipe to call his name three times. It was all a bit much, and I needed time to think. He said to take my time mulling things over as he pulled out my stack of 'art' magazines from under my bed. I turned my back and began to pick up my laundry as he laid his scale covered body across my comforter and unfolded his massive member.

That was a week ago. Today he informs me that if he can't feast on my mother's intestines then he really needs something else to eat. I called him so I have to take care of him. I ask what he wants. He thinks the innocence of babies or the broken dreams of the old sound tasty. Instead, I rattle off some menu items from Lardy Be's, the local greasy spoon, and he says that's close enough. Lardy Be's is good at two things: first, at deep frying everything in pig fat and secondly in unbiasedly offending those on either side of the religious fence. Through no fault of their marketing people, an equal amount of pandering and offensiveness left all the patrons unsure of their own feelings. The religious ones felt good about frequenting an establishment that references the Big Guy while the non-religious ones were moved beyond hilarity that 'said Big Guy' was a fry cook, using pig fat no less.

The vulgar eloquence is not lost on the demon as he lays across the order counter laughing and pounding his fist. After calming down, he declines the burger in favor of the chicken tenders because they remind him of... well, never mind what they remind him of. He dips them in loads of ketchup and moans so loudly with pleasure that I have a hard time getting my fries down.

My paltry allowance doesn't allow me to feed my demon at a restaurant every day, so I wonder aloud if maybe I can get an after school job. Shad, as I start calling him, says everybody knows that you have to maintain a certain grade level to get a job and being just to the right of 'idiot' disqualifies me. I tell him I feel hurt and demeaned. He says I should tell it to a fucking therapist.

With very limited routes to revenue and Shad becoming very insistent, I start boosting small things from the Gas-N-Go Mart for practice then promote myself to the Electro-Shack. I grab the kind of stuff that I can sell to 'those kids' at school. They were usually the ones I would avoid but now I go looking for them.

I hone my craft at different types of stores but I prefer the ones on the other side of town to avoid running into someone I know. Even so, one ill-fated day I hear, "Well, if it isn't little D.J. Freeman. What are you doing here?" as I'm about to liberate a few items from a pharmacy.

Dammit, it's Mrs. McCafferty, a bag of bones from my mother's old book club. No one's even called me D.J. in years. We exchange pleasantries but then she has to ask why I'm so red in the face.

I choke out a smooth reply about being there to purchase condoms. My hope is to throw her off my criminal intent and I fully expect her to grab her pearls and run from the store but I'm nauseatingly wrong.

"When did you stop shooting puppy water?" she laughs. "If you ever want to learn a thing or two, just point your little squirt gun my way, Daniel."

I clutch my own pearls as she walks out of the store with a little too much sway in her boney hips. I'm disgusted, not with her, but with the tightness in my crotch as I wonder if she wouldn't mind doing it with a bag on her head.

The money keeps Shad in Tender Pieces of (never mind) but he is growing impatient with me. He thinks that if I had any tenders of my own, then I could do better. I say 'fuck you' and he smiles at me. I throw up a little in my mouth and leave the room.

Funny thing about having your personal demon waiting for you when you get home; you really don't feel the need to be a jerk most of the day. I pay attention in class because it keeps my mind off the way Shad picks things from under his toenails, stuff like maggots and moldy cheese, all while sitting on my bed. My mother is impressed by how I am vacuuming and changing my bedding on a regular basis. Shad normally stays home when I go to school but will pop by from time to time, usually, whenever I have some type of presentation or oral report. Even though I know everyone sees jeans and a tee, I have to say that standing buck naked in front of the class has steadied my nerves. Shad claims he stays home because high school is scarier than Hell but I think he just prefers to loaf around and jerk off to my art magazines. His jizz sticks to the ceiling over my bed forming stalactites that drip on me while I sleep. I don't sleep with my mouth open anymore by the way.

I speak nicely to everyone because I get enough of the bile Shad spews at me. Not the malicious speech kind of bile but the greenish-black shit from the gallbladder or wherever. I know it's not really there but I can still see the stream flow from his mouth and feel it splash all over me. And oh, the smell of it.

My stealing skills get better and better until the day comes when, 'one of those kids' at school tells me that I'm really cool and how would I like to deliver a package? Twice the money and half the work of stealing; a no-brainer. Shad is so proud of me that he doesn't make me watch my parents eat piles of rotting meat covered in camel spit at the dinner table. Sure, I know what kind of spit it is because the lovely butt end of said dromedary is always positioned directly in my face as streams of drool issue from its blubbering lips and cover my parents and their food. They can't understand why my appetite has diminished but most of my baby fat is gone.

The next Sunday morning I am awakened by my mother talking and laughing on her phone. Once a month she calls her sister who moved to Ireland. This always coincides with 'Beef Stew Day.' I dash out of bed to make sure I'm correct. Sure enough, there she is with all the ingredients on separate plates and a large skillet on the stove. Unfortunately, Shad is there too. He is wearing a frilly apron that says, 'Kill the Cook' and I don't know what to expect. I've told him again and again to leave Mom alone and he mostly respects that although I don't know why. Maybe even demons have moms. Her back is turned as she gets out the slow cooker.

"Please don't ruin beef stew for me man," I plead silently to him. Shad doesn't even look my way as he picks up a big carton of beef broth. He twists off the cap, sniffs the carton and pours it down the drain. Twisting the tip of his nose like a spigot, he refills the carton with yellowing liquid from one nostril then the other.

I want to not care and to walk away but I have to know what he's going to do next because he just threw the platter full of cubed stew meat down the disposal. Fumbling around under his apron, forked tongue sticking out a bit, he pulls out, you guessed it, his penis. He places the thick, scaly length on the platter and slices it into perfect one-inch chunks. I'm numb at this point.

The oil is heating in the skillet and Mom is about to spice the meat with Shad's new ingredients. I can tell they are his because, although the bottles say 'thyme' and 'marjoram', things are slithering and jumping around in them. The plate of flour is dumped out and Shad leans over it, scratching his head furiously allowing the plate to quickly refill with white flakes of demon dandruff. The spiced meat is dredged in this new flour and Mom places them in the oil. Browning the meat in evenly spaced batches takes time, so Shad moves on to other prep work. With the potatoes tossed, he bends at the knees and shits out three medium sized white turds. I know for sure they are meant to be the potatoes because they have actual eyes that he digs out before cutting them into eighths. The eyes roll around on the floor for a while and then gravitate towards my mother's legs and look up her skirt.

This wakes me from my daze and I shake my head and growl, "You must be the shittiest demon in the entire underworld, you…"

My mother wheels around with fire in her eyes. Oh God! That was out loud! "What did you say?" she yells without taking the phone away from her face.

Shad pauses mid-prep, to snicker and watch. "Uhhhh, I saaaid, 'You must be the prettiest Freeman in the whole damn world.' Seriously, you should always wear that color blue." I'm about to pass out but I see my mother smile a bit. She may not buy it but she has bigger battles.

Ten hours later, I fight back the nausea to grudgingly savor my heaping bowl of stew. I moan loudly as I masticate the cubes of Shad-beef and gleefully watch him shiver and slowly shake his head. The pride of grossing out my demon and the warmth of the stew both fill me.

I don't mind delivering the packages at first and Shad gets to sample some exquisite auras but some of those people make me wonder if stealing from the Electro-Shack was better. One day, this guy I just gave a package to gives me a gun. He tells me it is not even loaded but sometimes a guy in my position needs to brandish. He calls me 'righteous'.

Shad is so pleased with me for earning the gun that he puts back the walls around the bathrooms at home and at school. It's such a literal relief to go to the bathroom without the demonic jeers and whistles and especially without ten Shad-faced cheerleaders, pom-poms and all, surrounding me and cheering 'Go, Go, Go!'

I know the gun's not loaded, 'cause that guy said so', but it still scares me. I don't know where the safety is or how to check the chamber and I want to look that up on the internet but Shad stops me. He whispers that the government is monitoring the web for just that kind of nefarious activity as he slaps foil hats on both of us. He might be right, so I just look at myself in the mirror holding the gun and take a selfie.

Dad sits me down to talk about how distant I am lately. He's glad my grades are going up and I look trim and fit but he's afraid something is going on with me. Shad thinks it's funny to lie on the back of the couch next to a tiki torch and sip my dad's brain fluid through a bendy straw. I tell my dad I'm fine and I love him so please don't worry. The love thing throws him for a loop and he just wanders away, with a bendy straw sticking out of his skull.

There is a weird thing happening at school. Ever since I started mingling with 'those guys', 'those girls' started noticing me a little. Nothing much at first, just the occasional side eye instead of the usual no eye. One in particular, Jaqui With a Q, has talked to me a few times. One day she comes up to me in the lunch line and tells me that the gym teacher, Mr. Crowder, will be out tomorrow and she has a key to his office. She tells me her father is out of town and I interrupt with, "Jesus, Crowder is your dad?"

Her perfectly threaded brows knit the word 'Idiot' and the word is echoed by her flawlessly lined lips. She informs me that our illustrious gym teacher is banging her mom so every time her dad goes out of town, the prick calls out. She made a copy of his key months ago in case she needed... sports medicine. She then invites me to either meet her in Crowder's office at lunch tomorrow or to join her and her family on the Dr. Ned show to help them all talk about their fucking feelings. I pick the former and hurry home after school.

This is the first time that I've called a 'me and my demon meeting' but I have a sheet of notebook paper with a bullet pointed list and hope not to go off topic. Shad sits on my bed, legs crossed, one knee clasped in his laced fingers, horned rimmed glasses dangling on the tip of his nose. He tries to look attentive as I clear my throat and bang my fist on the dresser to call the meeting to order.

Point 1: I am a virgin, as Shad most certainly knows. He nods furiously as I say we can agree that that is not a good situation with virginity being pure and all.

Point 2: My criminal activity has increased my fuckability. A real live female has expressed interest in me. Shad interrupts to question if this might not be some sort of joke or prank, i.e. involving pig's blood and laughter.

The truth is, I confess, there has been a definite shortage of blood to my brain since said offer was extended and that possibility had not crossed my mind. That being said, I would gladly give up my dignity or my home for the chance to get any part of me in, on, or around any part of Jaqui. Shad is nodding in agreement again and I start to feel hopeful.

Point 3: The real heart of the matter, I beg Shad to stay home and to not intrude on the 'date'. I beg him to not watch, cheer, laugh, touch, stroke or jack-off in the corner. To just, for the love of God, just NOT.

He promises, but I have to wonder what that is worth.

Like the end of a tunnel in an ever expanding hallway, reaching Crowder's office is mentally and physically grueling. While half expecting to open the door to an explosion of confetti and jeering schoolmates, I was caught much more off guard by the sight of Jaqui sitting on the desk pouring over a calculus textbook and jotting down notes. Derivatives tumbled off the book and down her perfect Cartesian form. Having exhausted my calculus vocabulary, I look in awe at her fabulous figures; legs for miles, skirt for inches, breasts for... something about circumferences and stuff about pi and then that face. Oh God, that face was shouting orders at me while I was lost in my Mesmer. She slams the book closed and points to the ancient sofa freshly lined with extra-large gym clothes. I saunter over to it and hold my hand out to her hoping for a tender moment to deliver the romantic words I've been practicing for about twenty hours. Instead, she plops a condom in my palm and orders me to hurry up cause she has a test next period. I'm glad she has one, since Mrs. McCafferty left me unable to purchase condoms, maybe permanently.

I damn near say, 'Yes Sir' as I peel my clothes off and lay down fumbling with the package, hoping like hell that I don't fold under the pressure. She easily peels off her scant clothes but doesn't take her bra off, just lifts her breasts out of the silky cups and that is the sexist thing I have ever seen and I don't have to worry about folding anymore. When she straddles me and glides onto my dick, I am transported to a place my hand has never taken me. I'm way too close to cumming way too quickly when I see the unimaginable; Shad's face playing across Jaqui's own, dancing in and out, swirling and fading.

I can feel myself softening even as she rides to her own climax. I have to think fast but, probably because of the condom, the only thing that comes to mind is the encounter in the pharmacy with Mrs. McCafferty. I try to dislodge one of the gym clothes we are laying on but none give and the only other thing within my reach are my own clothes puddled on the floor. I blindly reach down and come back up with my underpants. My tee shirt would have been better but I'm heading for a total collapse and have no time to be choosey, so I slap my boxers on the poor girl's shocked head, grunting quietly that it's just a 'thing' and to please, please go with it. After a few tense moments, she grudgingly resumes bouncing but with one eye and her nose sticking ridiculously through the opening of the plaid prison.

I slam the front door and walk into the living room where my father is sitting on the couch reading with Shad next to him. They are wearing matching faded blue robes and nursing identical bottles of decongestant. I scream out, "I thought you were going to stay home!"

They both say in perfect unison, "I've been home all day." My father looks shocked but I think he's just tired of trying to figure me out. Shad on the other hand, has a puzzled look on his face and some jacked up form of sincerity. In a split second, I know, without a doubt, that Shad appearing over Jaqui's face was all me. I head straight to the toilet and puke until the dry heaves drop me to the cool tile.

I welcome the routine of my next package delivery, but it's to a really bad part of town with something worse than the location going on. The guy's hair is all wrong if you can believe that. He's asking too many questions and I just want to leave, but he opens the package and offers me a sample. I decline and start to leave then... it happens so fast... he reaches into his jacket and I pull out the gun (for show) as he pulls out something black and I flinch, the gun goes off and there he is down on one knee, cursing with his badge covered in blood because I just shot off one of his fingers. He already used his other hand to get out his gun. I drop mine and scream like the honest to God little bitch that I am. I can't tell which is worse; having him point his gun at me or knowing I've been carrying around a loaded gun with the safety off just inches away from my dick.

The courts make an example out of me: shooting an officer, drug dealing and the BS of being a minor for one more month. The trifecta of screwed is what I get from the courts.

Shad is really upset with me. I thought he would have loved prison, but he tells me that the prisons are not just overcrowded with inmates but with damned demons. Some are personal demons that have been called and are attached to someone, but mostly they are just chop-licking visitors, aura sniffing and waiting. He can't turn a corner or drop a bar of soap without meeting so and such demon who knows his mother or cousin from whenever and he is so pissed, even for a demon.

I promise him I'll break out, but since I have no experience I wait until I hear these other guys talking about making a break for it. I thought they let me in on the plan because they felt sorry for me, but it turns out I am just the slow, stupid kind of distraction they need to help them get their plan to work. The guards catch me in minutes. The courts add time onto my sentence and the guards add ass-kickings onto my day. Shad is getting antsy. He tells me that killing a guard is a 'Get Out Of Jail Free' card. I tell him that I have morals and won't kill anyone. He thinks for a while and then suggests I call Big Melvin the 'N' word. I don't like that one either.

Every manner of human filth is in this prison and I beg Shad to leave me alone and take one of them. He says no problem, if I can get anyone to say his name three times.

I try it a few times, but none of these guys have a sense of humor. I'm covered in bruises.

It took some probing but Shad finally admitted that if I die of natural causes without being Core-worthy, then he would have to release me. He doesn't like this one at all because he says just because he's immortal is no reason to waste his fucking time.

I tell him, I'm young and can be rehabilitated as my lawyer says. I'm going to get out of jail, lead a virtuous life and live to one hundred and fifty just to screw with him.

He pats my head like I'm a child saying, he doesn't believe in legal mumbo jumbo and that we all die in a prison of our own making.

I tell him, he's a poet or at least what poets shit out. When he says fuck you, I just smile at him. I don't know if he throws up in his mouth but he calls me one sick puppy and heads for the showers.

Life is getting really hard for me and in my angst, I finally give up and decide to end it all. I walk up to Big Melvin in the cafeteria and sling the barely audible word 'Neanderthal' in his face. He looks down at me and shouts, "Boy, what did you call me?"

I drop, cover my head and yell, "That's right, I just called you the N word Big Melvin, now what?" I wait for the shoe or the shiv but instead there is rich, deep laughter. Big Melvin hauls me up, slaps me on the back then takes me to the chaplain and offers me as an Altar boy.

Praying makes me feel better and working with the chaplain helps me keep my head down for so many years.

Upon my release, I join the divinity school for The First Community of Reformed Sinners. They are not as fussy as some of the other religions. My first gig is working in what is labeled a troubled part of town. Shad is still waiting for me to do something Core-worthy.

Every day I hear, "Forgive me, father, for I have sinned."

To today's guest, I reply, "We all have, my son. Go on." The ketchup drips off my chin as I shovel chicken nuggets into my mouth.

A drop of freezing liquid falls on the top of my head and I look up to see Shad salivating at the sight of the guy's aura, I've seen that look before.

The guy tells me he had to 'take out' a mom and kid to send the dad a message. "Not like I wanted to, but ya' know, orders." I look at Shad and we smile.

I tell the guy to say ten Holy Hails and three Shaddafocups.

He asks me what a Shaddafocup is and I tell him it's Latin for extra forgiveness. He needs extra forgiveness I tell him. He agrees.

As he says the third Shaddafocup, Shad hugs me, flies through the lattice and drags the piece of garbage down to the Core. I'm alone and happy. Except, there is a putrid smell filling my nostrils. Dammit, Shad didn't tell me I would be able to smell my own aura. Maybe it was a rule he forgot to mention or maybe it was his idea of a parting gift. Either way, guess I'll get used to it.

I dip the last nugget in ketchup, rest my head on the

back wall of the confessional and look heavenward.

As I lift the nugget to my smiling lips, a drop of ketchup falls on my collar.

Oh, Hell. It's never going to be white again anyway…

-END

To learn more about the author, Maxine Kollar, find her author bio at http://www.grivantepress.com/

P.A.C.D. THE KITCHEN OF TOMORROW, TODAY!
By R.A. Goli

"You can open your eyes now."

Melanie frowned when she saw the renovated kitchen. She stared, mouth agape at the space-aged looking installation. Gone were the wooden cupboards with their wrought iron handles and the open shelves that held her recipe books and collection of mismatched glass bottles. Replaced by sleek and shiny glass and silver.

"Surprised?" Mike asked.

"Um, yeah. Shocked would be more appropriate," she said. Then turned to face her husband.

"It's your anniversary gift. That's why I sent you to the spa this weekend, so they could install it," he said, beaming.

"Uh, thank you, but why did we need a new kitchen? I loved the old one. It had personality, charm. This looks like it came from a spaceship," she said as she turned to look at the kitchen again.

"I know but you'll love it. This is more than a kitchen. This is your Personal Automated Culinary Droid. Come, I'll show you," he said as he grabbed her hand, pulling her towards a tablet that was fixed to the wall. He started swiping and tapping at the screen, his fingers moving too fast for her to follow.

"Slow down! I can't tell what you're doing," she said, her irritation increasing, though Mike remained oblivious.

"Sorry, sorry, I'm just excited," he said. "So I'm just going to set it to do a simple recipe so you can see it in action. Then I'll show you all the features."

A few more swift movements, he hit 'enter', then grabbed his wife's shoulders and spun her towards the kitchen. Mike had measured out the ingredients and arranged them on the bench in individual bowls. She watched as a pair of robotic arms came into view from a panel in the back wall, descending to the kitchen bench. The arms meticulously diced onion and pancetta, sliced mushrooms and tomatoes, and chopped parsley and basil, placing each item back where it had come from. Next, it grated cheese, then cracked eggs into a bowl, whisking them with a finesse she was surprised a machine was capable of. It turned on the stovetop and scooped up a knob of butter with a spatula, placing it into a waiting frying pan. Melanie watched, enthralled as the culinary droid fried onion, added the pancetta, then tossed in the vegetables and herbs.

"Is that a sensor?" she asked, pointing.

"Yeah, it has sensors in its hands and along the

bench. You have to get out the ingredients and in the correct quantities and put them on that sensor. That way the robot knows what to grab when and what it's supposed to do with it. You put them in order, see?" He moved forward and gestured for her to follow. She could see faint numbered lights on the sensor underneath the bowls. "It's also got a refrigeration mechanism under the sensor plates, so it will keep food cold for hours until it's ready to start cooking."

"So what's it cooking now?"

"Just frittata. I didn't want it to take too long. Should be ready in about half an hour," he said.

"But how does it know that, did you program the recipe in or something?"

"It comes with hundreds of recipes built in but you can also add your own. Either by uploading them to the database or punching them manually into the control panel," Mike said, the excitement in his voice evident. "So do you like it?"

Melanie nodded, mesmerized as the machine's arms drifted gracefully across the stove and bench top, placing ingredients into the frying pan and stirring it with care. Mike was trying. Clearly, this extravagant gift was to make up for the fact that they had grown a little distant lately, both working long hours. This at least would give them some extra time in the evenings. She turned to him and smiled.

"I think it's great. I for one am sick of coming home and eating take out or cooking at nine p.m. Thank you," she said and threw her arms around his neck, giving him the most passionate kiss she had in months.

The droid continued, adding the egg and cheese, tilting the pan to ensure the egg mixture covered the vegetables. After about ten minutes, it turned on the grill and placed the pan underneath to cook the frittata's top. Once it was lightly golden, the robotic arms removed it from the grill, cut it into wedges and transferred two slices each onto waiting plates. They sat at the dining table eating and watching as the droid arms cleaned up. It put the dirty dishes in the inbuilt dishwasher and wiped the surface of the bench down. Once the kitchen was clean, the dishwasher started, and the arms retracted back into the wall.

Later, when Melanie climbed into bed next to her sleeping husband, she felt closer to him than she had in a long time. She watched his peaceful face, and the rise and fall of his chest; pleasantly surprised by the unexpected tingling between her legs. They had both been too busy and too stressed to be intimate, and she hadn't wanted to. But now, as she traced her fingernails gently down his chest and stomach, and watched his cock slowly awaken, she felt slick with want. Her attentions woke him.

He smiled at her, then rolled to his side leaning on one elbow and snaked his other hand between her legs, running his knuckle over the wet material. She rolled onto her back, spreading her legs for him, while he teased her, stroking her center, and then moving his fingers away. She became impatient as her arousal grew.

"Ung, Mike…"

He grinned down at her, then slid his penis deep inside, his muscular body pressed against hers. They both moaned as he entered her, and Melanie thrust her hips up to meet him. He swirled his thumb around her clitoris as he fucked her and was polite enough to let her come first. Her breath quickened and her body felt flushed as the waves of pleasure spread from her aching clit and throughout her body. When she cried out his name, he could no longer hold on and shuddered in his own climax.

Weeks passed, and they both grew busy. Time moved ever forward and soon it had been six months since he had last touched her. Not only was Melanie missing the sex, but she was also becoming resentful. It annoyed her that he thought buying her an expensive automated cooking machine was enough to fix any problems in their marriage. She knew he loved her, and she understood that he had a stressful job, but she had needs too!

Though she was supposed to be at work, she had called in sick, wanting to spend some time alone, indulging her bad mood. She walked into the kitchen to make a cup of coffee. Mike, assuming she would have also been at work today had already set out the ingredients for the evening's dinner. Beef, a variety of peeled and measured vegetables ready for chopping, as well as a selection of sauces in small bowls. She didn't have to look at the control panel to know it would be a stir-fry. Plus the wok sitting on the unlit stovetop gave it away. It was already afternoon and feeling the way she was, Melanie decided she would have the droid make some cookies or something sweet. She went to the control panel and looked through recipes, her annoyance at her husband simmering beneath the surface of her thoughts.

As she scrolled through, an idea formed in her mind. A wicked idea that caused her to giggle like a schoolgirl. Now being adept at the culinary droid's controls, she invented a new recipe where the machine would have to cream butter and sugar with one hand and knead dough with the other. She programmed the positions of the robotic arms and the timer. "Twenty minutes should do it," she said, giggling again. Then she moved the dinner ingredients and wok down the end of the bench and stripped. Once naked, she tossed her clothes over the back of the sofa, grabbed her phone and positioned herself on the bench. Though she had turned off the refrigeration, the bench's coolness caused her nipples to harden, her skin erupting in goosebumps. She pressed start on the P.A.C.D. app, placed the phone on the bench beside her, and watched as the arms emerged from the wall above her.

She opened her legs in anticipation, already wet as she watched one arm move to her chest and the other grab a plastic stirring spoon. She had to wriggle down the bench a little to get the positions right, but when she did, she felt the cold metallic fingers of the hand knead her breast. The spoon lowered and began it's mixing motion, hitting her mound every half second. She raised her knees and thrust her vagina upwards, her wet folds opening and putting her clitoris on display. Now as the spoon mixed, it nudged her right on the sensitive nub and she squirmed against it. It took a while for her to become accustomed to the rhythm, but once she had, she could feel her orgasm building ever so slowly.

She closed her eyes and let her fantasies run free. She imagined there were random drunk men fondling her breasts roughly and she would squirm from side to side so that the robot hand would massage each breast in turn. She pretended that she was tied up and that various women were each taking a turn to lick her cunt, while men stood by, with dicks in hand, watching and wanking. Her clit ached as blood rushed to the tiny nub and each time the spoon hit, she was a little closer to release. Her orgasm came quicker than she had expected and was much stronger than any she'd had before. Waves of pleasure crashed through her body, so intense that her vision blurred. Because the spoon didn't stop when she was done, it brought her to another climax and then another until she reached back and grabbed her phone to stop the recipe. She lay there, exhausted and elated in a post-orgasmic haze, and soon drifted off to sleep.

The pain shot through her and she woke up confused and screaming. Her midsection was covered in blood and there was a large butcher's knife coming down again, trying to saw through the meat of her thigh. She screamed once more and attempted to get up, but the droid hand that wasn't grasping the knife was holding her down. Her arms flailed about as she tried to grab the blade before it plunged into her again, but her hands, slick with blood failed to keep it from stabbing down. A hollow wail emanated from her throat as it jabbed her. She tilted her head and reached out to grab her phone but as she did, the knife sliced into her belly, causing her to crumble inward. Knowing the only way to stop it was to get her phone; she desperately extended her arm for it once more.

So close, she stretched her fingers a little further and flicked the cell towards her. The thick coating of blood on the bench caused the phone to spin and slide and she watched in horror as it dropped over the edge, crashing to the floor.

"Nooooooo!" Angered and desperate she grabbed the metal arm that was pinning her down and tried to break it. It was far too solid, but she managed to lift it enough that she could maneuver her bloodied torso from underneath. The arm then moved up easily and continued backward behind Melanie's line of sight. She sat up and then felt the iron of the wok smash the back of her skull. Everything went black, and she crumpled back onto the bench.

Mike was in a good mood when he finished work. Having programmed the P.A.C.D. from the app before he left, he knew that their stir-fry would be ready when they got home. As he opened the door, the acrid smell of burnt meat stung his nostrils. He frowned as he hung his coat, his confusion deepening as he listened to the unnatural sound the normally whisper-quiet dishwasher was making.

What he saw when he walked in was not the stir-fry dinner and clean kitchen he had expected but a blood-soaked nightmare. The walls were splattered with gore, the floor covered in blood and scattered pieces of severed limbs. The robotic arms wiped the bench, knocking more pieces of his wife to the floor. The meat continuously splashed into the crimson puddle, creating a delicate pink mist, floating a few inches above the tiles. The wok on the stove was full of cooked meat, but not the beef he had set out earlier that day. He could see clumps of hair and bone, and several fingers; the bright pink nail polish and wedding ring glinting under the down lights.

A chortled moan escaped his throat, and he doubled over and heaved up the contents of his stomach, the bile mixing with her blood. He stumbled to the tablet and stopped the recipe, then fumbled with his phone to call the police.

Scrolling through the tablet, trying to understand how this gruesome scene had happened, he saw that the recipe was the one he had programmed. Baffled, he swiped to the meal before and saw the unusual recipe that Melanie had entered. She had named it 'Melanie's Special Recipe', and had listed the method of kneading dough and mixing butter and sugar, but had failed to add any other ingredients or instructions. His mind raced as he put the pieces together. When he caught sight of her clothes thrown over the back of the sofa, the puzzle was complete.

"No," he said to himself, shaking his head in disbelief. "*She* was the ingredient."

Now he understood. She had programmed the recipe intending to have the droid arms pleasure her. Then he had started the stir-fry. He had killed her. Or had she killed herself? He wasn't sure, but he stabbed his fingers against the tablet, deleting Melanie's recipe. Then poured himself a scotch, downing it in two large gulps. He grabbed Melanie's clothing and threw them into the hamper.

Returning to the living room, he refilled his glass and paced as he waited for the police. He knew they would ask why his wife was naked, but he could tell them that she often cooked naked. Surely that wasn't so unusual.

After a few minutes, he took his phone out and dialed the pre-programmed number for the Personal Automated Culinary Droid customer service. He tapped his foot anxiously while he waited for a connection.

"Hello, P.A.C.D. customer service, how may I help you?"

"Um, yeah, my name is Mike. I bought a Culinary Droid about six months ago and it's malfunctioned. I'd like to discuss getting a refund."

-END

To learn more about the author, R.A. Goli,
find her author bio at http://www.grivantepress.com/

ARABICA
By Cobalt Jade

A coffee shop: polished counters, well-worn stools, and walls covered with art showing the history of the city she lived in. Or had once lived in… her memory was not clear on that point.

She only knew that she saw it and could not move her head to look away.

Her sense of proprioception, the one that measured body position and posture, told her she was kneeling behind the counter at a raised level, arms frozen to her sides. This might have alarmed her, but she felt as lazy and pliable as a baby in its crib. All emotion had been scrubbed from her.

Out of the dreamlike silence came the scuff of a shoe on polished laminate. A young man appeared in front of her, dreadlocked and tattooed, his earlobes stretched by plastic disks. He held a rag in one hand. Businesslike, he began rubbing her breast with it.

Hey, stop that, she thought. Her throat vibrated, but

the words did not come out. Not even the anger did, only a dull sense of outrage. She could only kneel, paralyzed, as he rubbed her belly, her thighs, between her legs.

Oh! The jolt of sensation energized her. Her clit throbbed expectantly. How often had she met lovers in these places, drinking latte after latte or frozen macchiato in the summer? Drinking until the buzz threatened to send her into space with the top of her skull blown off, so horny she might tear off her dates' clothes then and there. Mostly men, but a few girls.

The rag withdrew. She felt more awake and more aware. She also knew she was naked, and could think of no reason she should be, or why she was in this coffee shop in the first place.

The barista — for he could only be that — reached behind her. He touched something at the back of her neck, the small hollow where her spine ended and skull began. Something wedged between her buttocks, filling her anus, vibrated with quiet power, sending energy throughout her body.

Am I dreaming? But it felt too vivid to be a dream.

The young man turned from her to fumble at her right. She heard water splashing into a sink. He returned to her with a pitcher and reached up. She felt something grind against her skull in circular motions.

With alarm she felt the water course down inside of her as if she were hollow and being filled. It pooled somewhere in her innards, giving her the sensation of having to piss and void her bowels at the same time. Not completely uncomfortable, but just a little urgent. A second screwing sensation tickled her scalp, and the barista stepped away. Still trapped in her motionless state, she felt him open the door to this place. A line of customers entered, college kids, entrepreneurs, people on their way to work either in offices or lofts downtown.

The young man came back to the counter.

"What'll it be for you today?" he asked the first.

"Latte Grande, make it a double."

A warm sensation built in her pelvis, pleasant. Almost as if…

Wait, wait, WAIT!

The scene froze like one of those commercials where the action stills yet remains three-dimensional. But one of the patrons did not. Seeming to notice her mental plea, he walked around to the back of the counter where she knelt next to the sink, and stood in front of her. He wore a business suit and overcoat, the type of man she saw every day on the bus.

"Are you having second thoughts?" he asked.

She could only stare at him, dumb.

He sensed her amazement and shook his head, amused. "Excuse me. Are you having second thoughts, *Katelyn Grohl?*"

The sound of her name galvanized her, made her aware of why she was there.

"You said the magic words, *wait wait wait,*" he reminded her smiling. "That was what we had agreed on, remember?"

Katelyn remembered. *I know. I am just questioning this whole scenario,* she thought, since she could not speak.

"You needed to kick the caffeine addiction for your health," Dr. Sumter, said. "It's negative reinforcement. We went over all this before the <u>Immersion</u> began."

I know, I know, it's just that...

"It wasn't what you expected? Remember your mind fills in the details, just as you are giving me some form to speak to you in your dream."

But it seems to be getting... Katelyn wasn't sure how to put it. The scenario was erotic, definitely, but she hadn't discussed her sexual behavior with him. Only the coffee addiction.

"Whatever is happening, remember it's your doing, not mine. If you like, though, we can abort."

She couldn't do that, she had spent far too much on the Immersion already. Her friends had reassured her it would work, telling her they had been cured of similar addictions.

There's something about it that seems sinister, she said.

"Of course there is. Remember we are attempting to change deep-seated, hard-wired behavior patterns. Addiction is never easy to overcome, whether it's opiates, overeating, or gambling. Resistance is to be expected."

Perhaps that was all it was, just resistance.

All right, she thought reluctantly. *Let it continue.*

Dr. Sumter blipped out, and the scenario, and the barista, came back into life.

The young man opened the refrigerator door to take

out the milk. In the brief reflection Katelyn saw a chrome-plated statue of a young woman on her knees, thighs parted, neck outstretched, lips pursed. Across her chest was a series of lit buttons and round dials, and between her legs, a metal grill and drain pan. On her head, a screw-on cap that looked remarkably like an old-fashioned bellhop's hat.

I'm an espresso machine.

A goddamn espresso machine.

Wait...

She got no further as the young man hooked a finger deep into where her navel would have been. She felt him pull and a part of her detached, almost as if it was a drawer. He removed a strainer cup and packed ground coffee into it, tamping it down, then replaced it and pushed the part back inside her. He poked at the buttons on her chest.

Her transmuted body came fully into service. Water boiled inside of her, filling her with heat. Mute and paralyzed, she grew increasingly excited... sexually excited... as the pressure built. The true horror of what her unconscious had done, what it had come up with as treatment for herself, sunk in. It had become its own entity now, carrying her along as a helpless passenger to fulfill the mental treatment she had signed for.

The pressure reached its climax, no longer pleasure but a hot, steamy torture. She saw red, then black. Just as she thought she would die, the climax came.

Aaaahhhh... Steam hissed out from between her lips as rich, dark espresso trickled and tickled between her legs. Pain became pleasure with the wonderful release. Then pain again as the barista yanked her breast down and immersed her nipple in a carafe of cold milk.

She would have shrieked if she could, but only hissed, as the super-heated steam tortured and pleasured her once again. Her second orgasm went on and on, the erotic sensations amplified by the swishing motions the manager made with the metal pitcher.

The barista lifted the mug from her pubic area and spooned the steamed milk into it, offering it to the customer.

Katelyn gave a wheezing sigh, the last wisps of steam escaping from her lips. The pleasure faded. She felt used up, sated, heavy. If she'd been human, she might have rolled over, grabbed the comforter, and fallen asleep.

But no, now there was another patron, and again her navel-cum-drawer was opened, cleaned, and packed with fresh coffee, the process beginning anew. Again, no strength to send out her plea. This time, the nipple of her other breast was pressed and aimed, forming a whipped cream cap on a white chocolate mocha, a lively mix of pressure, pain, and a sickly sweet release.

This is too much. Desperately she denied her addiction. *I don't want coffee. I don't need coffee. No coffee!*

But her mind became mush as another hellish orgasm came and went, her clit a button of nerves as the barista cleaned it with his rag.

Perhaps, she thought, when she could, *one addiction is being replaced by another?*

She screamed. The customers, though they did not

really exist outside her mind, heard it as a muffled hiss emitted from beneath her bellhop's cap.

If there is a hell, she thought, *this is it.* And forgot her own words, again, when one of her customers ordered a quad...

-END

To learn more about the author, Cobalt Jade, find her author bio at http://www.grivantepress.com/

TOILET MANNERS
By Eddie Generous

The stalls rose to a foot from the ceiling. Pine finished to golden shine, polished with a slick, seemingly wet, waxy sheen. The floor was of pale granite. The toilet paper was luscious two-ply.

Wade felt as if he could spend half the night in there.

He'd lowered his pants to appear a reasonable patron making likely use of the can instead of what he was. An emotionally wrought mess, killing time.

Wade was capricious in shades of self. Sometimes he was a furious man, awaiting the moment to bring the wrath. Other times he was a man uncaring, not a trouble, to hell with the stressors of life. Mostly, he was a sad sack, self-abasing thoughts and words loaded and ready.

Délices Rares was the fanciest place he'd ever been, and it made him sick. Being there, not the restaurant with its fine scents and sweet wine. It was either that his wife, Gabriela, did not recognize facts or that she just did not care. It began two years earlier and at first; it was for the good. Gabriela, a physiotherapist, worked alone besides her clients, but on the whole, worked for the province alongside a list of other physiotherapists.

Jamie, a physiotherapist from the mainland, met Gabriela at a conference. They gelled and Wade was happy that his wife had another friend. She was always one that enjoyed options. Wade himself was a loner and mostly fine with the fact, or at least, felt resigned to the fact.

A month after the conference, Jamie invited Gabriela on a camp-out with a few of the *girls*. Wade wished her well and ate a pizza from the freezer, as when he didn't have to cook for two, he didn't feel very much like cooking.

The afternoon following, Gabriela came home excited and red-faced. The *girls* had gone skinny-dipping, like teenagers. They had drinks and told stories. Jamie did Gabriela's toes in pink by lantern light within the canvas of their shared tent.

Stopping abruptly from her tale, Gabriela had demanded, "Let's fuck!"

It had been a few weeks, the norm, and if hanging out on a camp-out put Gabriela in the mood for physicality, Wade thought she ought to go off every weekend.

The sex was dutiful. Two people mashing together toward mutual fluid release. It was as it always had been.

After slipping off to the can attached to their bedroom, one after the other, and then returning to retrieve their clothing, Wade finally asked, "Does Jamie have a husband?"

"Oh no, she's a lesbian... single either way," said Gabriela.

Thinking back made Wade shiver. Reminiscing on pain was no way to kill the slow clock working in the back of his head. On the toilet in the fancy restaurant where his wife, her girlfriend and another couple sat awaiting apértifs, Wade pondered whether or not it was cuckold if the sexual intruder was another woman.

The restroom door wheezed and Wade listened to squeaky wet steps cross the floor, stop before his stall door a moment, casting a wide shadow and then open the stall door to his left. Wade had a sudden pang of embarrassed fear. Bad things often happened in toilets.

"In fine dining toilets?" he whispered and made dutiful sounds with the toilet paper rolls.

The swishy steps sounded strangely wide, short, barely lifting.

Go away. Go away, Wade thought. *Be a spring snowflake, melt away and let me be alone.*

The movement changed direction and Wade imagined an enormous fat man with varicose veins running up his dimpled thighs. Then an old man with a wobbly gait and boney knees. Or maybe, a small boy with his pants around his ankles holding onto his undies to fight the need until the porcelain bowl was safely beneath him. The make or model of humanity mattered nothing. Wade's private self-commiseration was no longer possible with another body in the room.

He stood, flushed for effect and lifted his pants,

facing the stall wall he shared with the other patron. In the short gap below the partition, a milk carton slid and banged against the finely finished wood. Wade had his hands on his shirttails, tucking them in and stopped curious at the movement. The toilet paper roll tink-tinked and swung on a screw sideways revealing a shadowy hole. The hole was just about big enough for a…

"Holy shit," Wade whispered, his heart pounding, terrified by the connotation.

"Hey you, you put something through and I'll put my mouth on it," said a soft deep voice. Lips sounding wet, as if salivating while speaking.

"What? No, I'm not gay," said Wade, heart fluttering, pants filling with the notion of a mysterious blowjob, of a tit-for-tat, of working toward evening the field. "I'm sorry."

Tit-for-tat…

The marital erosion had begun months earlier.

It was to be a good day. There were tickets for the Canucks until there weren't. Wade was to meet his old friend Walter in Vancouver to catch up and catch some hockey. Walter was one of three men that acted as groomsmen about a million years earlier for Wade and Gabriela's special day.

Unexpectedly, Walter called just before Wade made it past the outskirts of town and to the highway, explaining that they couldn't catch up after all. Walter's wife had come home from the doctor's office with sad, scary, all-encompassing news. The big C.

Wade turned around feeling terrible only to feel worse upon arrival back home. His wife and her lover in bed in what the kids in high school used to call *scissor action*. Rather than speak up, Wade backed out of the room and drove to the city. He parked north of the city and rode the SkyTrain for four hours before returning to his car and then home. Gabriela was on the couch next to Jamie, they smiled and giggled, made girly jokes, and Wade recognized that his cowardice to unwelcome change had paralyzed his tongue.

As of lately, Gabriela visited Jamie two nights a week, sleepovers, *you know the ferry schedule, what a pain in the ass!*

"What's gay about some head?"

"No, but… It's the men's room and…"

"Look, you can't see me. I can be anything you want. Come on, I'm quite skilled."

An image of Gabriela lapping at Jamie as a dog at a water dish flashed and, to his shock and giddy nervous energy, he let his pants fall. His penis tented the front of his shorts. The shorts followed his pants while hands held shirttails aside.

"I can't believe I'm doing this… Is it even clean…? Are you even clea—? Oh god, yes," his voice trailed off in ecstasy.

A new fantasy played over his mind, Gabriela, hog-tied, tears running. He held a gun to Jamie's head while she slurped and sucked. It was horrible, disgusting and all too erotic.

The mouth working his manhood received a quick splash and continued, on and on until Wade felt drained, his penis quickly softening.

"I know you're straight," said the voice after a loud swallow, "but, maybe you can suck, just a little. Even just the tip, rim it some, maybe?"

Surprising himself, feeling so good and thankful, Wade replied, "Just a little."

"Umm, good," said the voice.

Both sides adjusted, the milk crate slid aside while Wade dropped to his knees, eyes closed, a parade of butterflies in his guts.

Are you really going to suck cock! asked the voice of Gabriela in his mind.

Sure, what's it to you? he thought back to the voice. *It's a new world, nothing to be ashamed of!*

"You still there?" asked the voice.

Wade reached up and grabbed the semi-rigid shaft, extended his tongue to the tip, his mind filling in blanks where his eyes refused to see. It was odd. The head was concave at the center and the ridge of the head sloped like a megaphone.

You're licking an uncircumcised penis.

It was a shock. He expected the penis to be like his own. The intrigue and fun flooded away, slipping down the floor drain of that fine restaurant.

His eyes opened as he said, "I'm sorry. I can't... What the hell?" Wade leapt back against the opposite dividing wall.

The thing before him, poking through the hole was ghostly whitish yellow, six inches long and definitely not a penis. On the floor where the milk crate had sat was a globule form, fat and the same ivory shade as the...

Tentacle? Antenna?

"Oh Christ! Oh Christ!"

"Quiet! They'll hear, now do what you're told. Trust me, you don't want me over there."

Wade clicked the latch and swung open the wonderfully finished stall door. The stall door next-door squeaked open as well.

"Your mouth or your nethers," said the deep voice, no longer so smooth. "Makes no difference to me and it's going to happen one way or another."

"That's not right, that's not..." *fair. One way or another... Tit-for-tat is better than the alternative.*

The stall door squeaked closed and the latch clicked.

"Good boy," said the voice.

Eyes closed, Wade imagined Gabriela and Jamie holding six-shooter pistols with pearl handles and gold on sterling inlay designs to his head. Laughing, their breath smelling of wine and a fishy, pussy scent. Their bodies red with rubbing and their hair matted from exertion.

Wade felt a stringy splash at the back of his throat. Like saltwater chalk.

"Don't you dare stop!"

He didn't.

Wade, unthinking beyond a subconscious level, swallowed and burst out of the stall while the thing next-door sighed. Straightening his attire as he ran, Wade made it out of the salle de bain in time to pluck the final olive from the dish and spill the last bit of wine from the first décanteur into his glass.

"Did you fall in?" asked Jamie.

"No, there's a glory hole. I was getting a blowjob," Wade said absently. "Then it was my turn, tit-for-tat's all fair, right?"

Laughs all around.

The waiter returned. "Excuse me, we have now located the misplaced entrée and it shall be out momentarily. More sauvignon blanc?"

"Yes, yes," said Roger Washington, one of the couple Gabriela knew from one committee or another. "Best bring two unless something accents la limace? Bring what suits. How did you misplace an entrée?"

The waiter shrugged, "Big, busy kitchen. I know the very wine for the delicacy," he said and then departed.

Wade drank the wine and then his water, light-headed and confused. Feeling filthy. Zoning away. Abashed, he felt the heat rise within. What he'd done was disgusting, cowardly, insane.

"La limace!" the waiter's voice echoed over the table conversation and Wade finally came back to the real world. Two men set a silver platter on the table and lifted the domed cover revealing an enormous ivory slug. "The tentacle is said to hold aphrodisiac powers," the waiter grinned at Roger and then at Wade. "And with some," the waiter spied the women, lifting his brows, "a calcium deposit solidifies in the heat of the pot and becomes a precious p..."

Wade stared at the two-foot slug, boiled now. He felt a sickness rising, a wave of slug ejaculate inching up his throat. He'd gone green.

"Wade, you feeling all right?" asked Gabriela.

"Little slug make you sicky?" Jamie mocked.

Wade dry-heaved.

"Uh-oh," Jasmine Washington said from behind a palm.

Wade lurched again. And again. And once more. Wine, olives and a single white pearl splashed down. The bead pinged against the china and rolled with the puddled ooze spilling onto the fine white linen.

-END

To learn more about the author, Eddie Generous, find his author bio at http://www.grivantepress.com/

THE STRAY
By Calypso Kane

Everett supposed it wasn't too odd he'd fallen into this routine. He'd driven his parents crazy with his army of strays. Every skinny cat and bedraggled pup was welcome. He'd once given his mother a heart attack when he revealed a shoebox containing a garter snake. It had previously contained a frog with a bad leg. Everett had left it unattended to bring it some bugs and nature had taken its course. The snake was cooler anyway. His parents had forbidden him to have all these pets, divvying them up among animal shelters and backyard wildernesses as they saw fit.

In the present day Everett could only feed strays which made it to his fifth-floor apartment. He'd hung a bird feeder accordingly. As it happened, birds weren't the only fauna which traveled at that altitude and were keen to take handouts from the locals.

Enter the stray named Felix.

Or so the various notes claimed. Felix didn't possess

standard human vocal cords despite the otherwise mirrored anatomy. When he became vocal—sometimes to sigh, occasionally to laugh, often to bitch in varied inflections of distaste—it was with a surreal ululation of bass that made Everett's skull tremble like a tuning fork.

So Felix preferred to write. After burning through three packs of sticky notes in as many days, Everett had picked up a cheap whiteboard and a pack of markers. He'd left them on the TV tray near the backdoor one evening. Two hours later he'd heard the door open and then the stealthy scratching of a marker. Another minute passed before Felix came to him in the bedroom. That night had turned into an ecstatically exhausting one. In the morning the whiteboard was gone. It only returned with Felix's visits.

So it was tonight, with the whiteboard all but crushed against Everett's face. Written there was:

WHY BOXES?

This was in reference to the cardboard boxes lining the walls. Everett's shelves and cupboards were barren. He'd been dismantling a bookcase when Felix found him. Felix noted the screwdriver still in Everett's hand, frowned, stole the tool, and tapped the board with it.

Tap!

WHY?

TAP!

BOXES?

Everett held back a sigh.

"Because I'm leaving." Which he'd mentioned a

month ago. Each week. Every other night. He reached for the screwdriver. Felix grudgingly relinquished it. Before Everett could resume the whiteboard was in his face again.

WHERE? WHY? GONE HOW LONG?

"One county over. New job. Probably a very long time." Everett pushed the whiteboard away. There was a hasty scrubbing as Felix erased the message. Everett managed to pry two shelves loose before the whiteboard returned.

HOW LONG IS LONG?

"If things turn out the way I want, many, many years."

NO. NO YEARS. NO MONTHS. NO NIGHTS.

Another scrubbing, then a final declaration:

NO.

"Yes. I've worked very hard to get this position and the new place I'm going to has—,"

The whiteboard was pulled away, refilled, and swung back so quickly it nearly banged against his nose.

NO GOING. FELIX IS HUNGRY.

"And I'll feed you in a minute. Just let me finish th —*Felix*." The screwdriver was yanked away again. "Don't be a prick about this." Felix didn't break eye contact as he tossed the screwdriver under the couch. "You're going to be a prick about this."

Felix gave out a trill Everett had learned to take as a combination of *yes* and *fuck you.*

"You're making this a bigger deal than it is. If you want to keep up our routine, you can just come to the new place." Felix appeared to mull this over before sticking out his tongue. It was half as long as his arm and curled like a party favor. "Mature." Felix kept his tongue out as he raised his free hand. He laid his tongue between the fork of his index and pinkie. "Very mature." Again, the whiteboard:

VERY HUNGRY.

"I know. I'm finishing with the bookcase first. You can wait a minute." Everett moved past Felix and got on his belly to look under the couch. He was halfway through a thought about the ratty college remnant—*Better to leave the damn thing by the road*—when a hand landed on the seat of his boxers. Another stroked his back. "Not right now." Everett grabbed the screwdriver and tried to sit up. Felix pressed him back down. Fingers dipped under the hem of his undershorts. "Cute. Still not feeding you until the bookcase is done." The groping slowed. There was a pinch. "Come on." Felix pulled away. "Thank you." Everett returned to the bookcase.

As he knelt he went on, "The new place is actually a house. Not *much* of a house, more like a mailbox with a smaller mailbox out front, but it *is* a house. Which means no downstairs neighbors to give noise complaints, so, you know, automatic plus. Also there's a garage which means my poor little piece-of-shitmobile is less likely to be keyed by the local bored—,"

A familiar knob jabbed the back of his head.

"—asshole."

The knob retreated as its owner crouched behind him. Now the knob dug into his lower back. As the folklore declared, it was cool to the touch. Unmentioned in the lore was how warm the rest of the body was. Everett heard a fleshy shifting sound—it made him think unpleasantly of a giant popping his knuckles—as Felix undid his wings from their slots in his back. They folded around Everett in a doubled embrace, Felix's arms already being locked around his middle and plucking at the waistband of his Hanes. Everett was swaddled in a pocket of heat, skin, and hunger.

Everett poked a wing with the Phillips.

Felix grudgingly unwrapped himself. This was immediately followed by another grab for the screwdriver. Everett held it out of reach.

"You're going to wait longer the more you do this. Just watch TV or something."

Felix chattered under his breath in a tone that translated roughly to, *this is unfair, unjust, ungrateful, and I am too good for such malign treatment.* Then, as he sulked his way onto the couch, a parting grunt of, *you dick.*

"The feeling's mutual." The TV clicked on and Felix found a rerun of *The Twilight Zone.* That was good. Felix always enjoyed scribbling out litanies of criticism regarding the depiction of the show's monsters and waving them in Everett's face, as if Everett could somehow pass these grievances on to an undead Rod Serling. Half a year ago Everett had mentioned this aloud. Felix had offered a rebuking note:

ROD SERLING NOT DEAD. ONLY MOVED.

Everett had never mustered the nerve to ask where.

The current episode was, "Queen of the Nile." The

last time Felix watched it he had several notes' worth of criticism regarding how the actress looked nothing like Cleopatra herself—he knew, having met the ambitious young lady once before—and how this fake Cleopatra's aim for movie stardom was an absolutely disastrous choice for a creature of her intellect. Even the simpletons among immortals knew better than to make themselves famous. There were only so many ways one could explain away endless youth. Fake birth certificates only went so far before one had to change addresses and even that cliché was becoming trickier to pull off under the omniscient eyes of the technological age. Several creatures who'd lived among the mortals without a glamour were now moving back beyond the Veil rather than put up with the ceaseless scrutiny of documentation.

This time though, there was no commentary. Just Felix scowling at the colorless people until the actress, killed the reporter and Mr. Serling gave his parting warning to the audience. Everett kept his peace as well. So much so he did not bring it to Felix's attention he'd finished taking the bookcase apart well before the first commercial break. When Felix saw this, the scowl deepened.

"You seemed so invested." He saw the bones move in Felix's hand and a vein pulse in his arm, a twitch away from crushing the remote into plastic splinters. Everett stood up from where he'd sat cross-legged and revealed he'd somehow misplaced his boxers. The remote fell from limp fingers. "Still hungry?"

Felix was herding Everett into the bedroom before

the third syllable. There was a brief pause as the state of the bedroom was observed, littered with boxes and unmade furniture as it was. But the mattress was still in its frame and the nightstand stood by its side. Felix chucked Everett onto the bed and pawed through the nightstand's bottom drawer. Out came the half-emptied K-Y and lambskin.

Meal prep began.

More than once Felix had insisted on doing it all himself. He'd bound Everett's hands to the headboard a few times to punctuate this, citing the fact that:

THIS IS NOT FOR FELIX WHAT IT IS FOR EVERETT. FELIX EATS. EVERETT FEEDS. DOES NOT NEED TO MOVE.

'Move,' meaning joining in the foreplay. All the little touches, squeezes, and come-ons were superfluous to things like Felix, despite their infamous eating habits. To them, this was no more than milking a cow or seasoning a fillet. Still, Everett didn't much care for just laying there getting fondled. He'd made this clear after the third night of having his hands bound while Felix played with his food. Either he got to interact or Felix could find his supper elsewhere. Since then Everett had been free to paw at Felix and vice versa until it came time to eat.

Tonight Felix appeared to be in no mood for such play. Everett quickly found his lower half flopped over Felix's stiff lap. He received three swats on the ass in rapid succession. Felix barked something at the back of Everett's head and swatted him again. It was not enough to hurt, but the fact that he had lapsed into spanking at all was telling.

"… are we still on the moving thing?"

There was another curt *whap!*

"Look, if you're that wound up about it, this can wait. There's someth—*ow!* Alright, that one *stung*." Everett wrenched around as much as he could to glare. Felix returned the look. It softened a little as the swatting hand began to rub.

There was a soft droning that roughly resembled an apology. Everett let it go as well as any further talk of the move. It would be better to save the whole of it for when Felix's hunger pangs were satisfied and both parties were too worn out for further sniping. Felix seemed to be of a like mind as his next move was to turn Everett into a glove. Everett sent a hand between his legs to touch—enough to arouse, but not to finish. The longer the sensations lasted the more Felix got to eat. Something to do with the consumption of erogenous output or brain chemistry or the energy of spent life force or similar nonsense. Whatever it was, the sparks of positive response were appetizers to Felix and his kin. The orgasm itself was the equivalent of a sirloin steak.

That night, Felix had a whole cow's worth. Every time he finished with one position, Everett having come with blissful yelps of profanity, Felix would readjust him and start again. It didn't matter how many minutes it took for Everett to recoup, Felix remained attached to him, eager to prep the next serving. It got to the point where Everett was too exhausted to return the ministrations and simply let himself be operated like a flesh machine. Lips and neck, nipples and ribs, hips and cock, thighs and buttocks. Around and around again until Everett suspected that he was now physically incapable of walking in a straight line. As Felix was lining himself up for the umpteenth round Everett dropped the safeword.

"Check," he panted. "Ch-check. Check, please."

Felix gave a patronizing warble and delivered a last friendly slap to Everett's flank. When he left the bed Everett saw he was looking a bit ragged himself. Thinking on it, Everett couldn't recall the last time they'd engaged in such a marathon. Felix was usually full after three or four helpings. Sometimes only a peckish two. Now he was stooping, hunched over the bedside like a gargoyle. Everett heard a noise—the giant popping his knuckles again—and the image was complete. Felix's wings were out.

"You're going already?"

A nod.

"Please don't. Not yet. There was," he winced as he sat up, "something else I wanted to talk about. I wanted to ask…" *If you'd come with me to the house. Not to visit, but to stay. That's all I want to say, all I want to,* "… what are you doing?"

At that moment Felix was picking Everett up off the bed. A heartbeat passed in which Everett felt like those wilting damsels in silent movies, or—stupid, stupid thought—like a newlywed being carried over a threshold.

Felix promptly flipped Everett over his back like a potato sack. He hung awkwardly between the pulsing sheets of the wings, briefly stunned into silence. The silence died when Felix rushed down the hall, through the living area, and out the sliding back door at a sprint.

Felix's wings stretched wide in the summer moonlight.

"No. No, Felix, don't you fucking dare—,"

A last fleeting impulse of shame at the idea of being seen by the neighbors kept Everett's swearing down to a loud whisper as they launched into the sky. It was only when the complex's roof was shrinking below him that memory pierced his panic to remind him that Felix's kind could only be seen by those they wanted to see them. A handy trick. At least he wouldn't show up on any security cameras bare-assed and being spirited away by a priapic bogeyman.

On the downside, he was now losing sight of the city as it blended into one moonlit jigsaw puzzle of streetlights and highways, drawing closer to the stars.

"Felix what the fuck are you doing!? *Felix!*"

Felix's only answer was to tighten his grip on Everett's legs and give his backside a reassuring pat. Perhaps knowing this wasn't enough, he vocalized.

"*Vrrrl,*" he tried. "*Vrlll. Thrrw Vll.*" Finally, "*Thhrrrew Vallle.*"

"Veil?" *Threw vale?*

No.

Through Veil.

Like all the other creatures that couldn't be bothered with slumming among mortals any longer.

As they flew, Felix did his best to soothe his passenger. He stroked its legs, kneaded its hindquarters, and rubbed its kicking feet. He'd vocalize whenever the screaming hit a lull, the poor thing having made itself hoarse. This was always the rockiest part of adoption, he'd been told. It always took a while to rebuild the trust between master and pet after the latter had been plucked from their habitat, but they learned eventually. A few years if they were stubborn. Felix didn't mind.

He loved his stray too much to give up on it now.

-END

To learn more about the author, Calypso Kane, find her author bio at http://www.grivantepress.com/

THE OLD MAN IN THE SUIT
By Nicholas Paschall

The streets of New Orleans were awash with the lights and sounds of Mardi Gras, the torrid display of primal urges at every corner as men and women drank, ate and danced the night away. Endless parades of masked figures were dressed in bright and eccentric clothing, designed to tantalize the senses. The smell of sweat and lust hung heavy in the humid night air of the raucous city, as bars pulsed with the sound of music, entrancing drunken revelers in as quickly as they bled out onto the wild party of the street.

Behind a squat lesbian bar known simply as Red, two such individuals were taking advantage of the darkness of the cramped alleyway. Long alabaster legs with smooth cream-colored flesh were intertwined with mocha-colored hands and moist ruby lips, both women doing their best to chase away the demons of everyday life through heavy doses of tequila and the risqué act of making love so openly.

"Mmm... harder!" The blonde-haired woman

groaned, her ivory corset partially undone, the laced sides haphazardly unstrung enough for the garment to be pushed down over her ample breasts. Beads of sweat, interrupted only by trails of saliva, slid down her neck and into her cleavage as she gripped the kinky black hair of her lover, forcing her deeper between her legs.

Her lover merely smirked as she drove her fingers in faster. Jennifer loved picking up tourists during Mardi Gras; they were always so willing, so supple... so delicious. Allowing her head to be forced into the apex of the lewd woman's legs, set to the task of bringing about a toe-curling orgasm.

The woman lashed back her head, letting loose a throaty moan as she massaged Jennifer's scalp. Mewling in pleasure from the darting lashes of the ebony girl's pink tongue, savoring the rough texture with every pass from the slow strokes of the finger entering her. Sitting atop a garbage can, legs splayed open with her panties pulled to the side, the drunken blonde could scarcely believe she was allowing this to happen.

She could also scarcely think, thanks to the electrical jolts of pleasure firing through her body, the waves of passion that would ebb and flow over her drunken thoughts. She leaned back, one hand sliding up to grasp her left breast, the pressure of her impending orgasm mounting.

Licking up from the blonde's opening, Jennifer slid another finger in to join the first as she moved to suckle on her partner's right breast. Pulling on the nipple with her teeth and rolling it in her mouth, Jennifer lavished attention onto the woman as she picked up speed with her hand.

Jennifer let go of the nipple, a light popping noise leaving her lips as she leaned forward, resting her chin in the crook of the woman's shoulder.

"Are you going to cum for me, hmm?" She whispered sweetly, her tongue seeking out her victims' earlobe.

The blonde nodded shakily, not trusting herself to speak beyond the grunts and moans that were tumbling forth from her mouth. A throaty purr slipped past her lips, before she turned to Jennifer, desperately trying to catch her lips in a needed kiss.

Jennifer's hand stopped, her two fingers knuckle deep in the drunken girl. Her other hand snaked up the blonde's body, grabbing onto her chin and forcing her head to the side.

"Nuh-uh... no kissing for you." Jennifer chided before settling her mouth over the thrumming pulse of the blonde, sucking on the skin in a teasing manner. The woman moaned in both protest and pleasure, rocking her hips to try and get Jennifer to continue the torrid finger play on her flower.

Jennifer happily obliged.

Minutes passed by, the only sounds in the air the distant cry of trumpets from the bands and the agonized moans of the woman as Jennifer wrenched the last vestiges of pleasure from her body. Every time she approached orgasm, Jennifer would slow her hand, torturing her in an endless loop.

"Please... I need it!" The blonde moaned after what felt like hours, as her third approach to orgasm was halted by Jennifer's teasing ministrations.

Jennifer lifted her head from the blonde's throat, breathing into her ear. "Need what darling?"

"I need... to cum!" The woman gasped, shuddering as Jennifer curled her fingers within her. "Please just let me cum!"

"Yeah," Drawled a voice from the darkness, causing both women to jump, "Let her cum girl, then she can do you next."

The blonde began hastily rearranging her outfit, sliding back far enough on the garbage can lid for Jennifer's fingers to slip out of her. Jennifer turned, glaring around as she did, her eyes wide and angry.

"Who the fuck is there?" She hissed, trying to locate the speaker, only to curse at the shadows of the alleyway.

Emerging partially from the darkness, a lean elderly man smiled at Jennifer. "No need to stop, it was just getting good!"

"Get the hell out of here you freak!" Jennifer growled, turning towards her drunken friend. "I'm so sorry; we should have gone to a hotel or something."

"I should really get going..." She slurred, stumbling to her feet as she buckled her skirt back into place, her face flushed and red. Waving her hands, she brushed away Jennifer as she slipped through the back door of the bar.

Jennifer growled as she turned, glaring at the smirking man.

Face lined with heavy wrinkles and eyes covered by black spectacles, the man had snow white hair. Wearing a three-piece suit with sparkling white buttons sewn onto black silk, the lean figure looked every bit the part of a wealthy tourist. In his left hand was a black cane topped with a yellowed skull, twin glimmering black stones set deep into the sockets. He obviously had the cane purely for decoration as he moved with the fluid grace of a dancer.

"I like your bravado girl, as well as your taste in women," The man said, glacial eyes peering over the shaded spectacles. "How much would it cost to get a treatment like the young ladies?"

"I'm not a whore!" Jennifer spat, eyes looking longingly towards the back door where the object of her affections had fled to. "Besides, I only like real men when I decide to swing that way."

"I'm more than you could handle child, trust me on this," The man replied, placing his cane in front of him, both hands resting on the skull. "So, how much for a night?"

"Fuck off," flipping him the bird, she stormed out of the alleyway and onto the street, "Go to hell old man!"

The old man smiled as he inclined his head and stepped back into the darkness of the alleyway. "To Hell, it is then…" he muttered, just loud enough for her to hear.

Ignoring him, she strode off down the well-lit sidewalk, grumbling about her own needs as she felt her throbbing core ache between her thighs. "Perverted old man ruined all of my fun! And I didn't even get to get off!"

Stalking past an open-air bar, a live band playing a swinging jazz song, Jennifer decided to stop and try to take her mind off the problem. Maybe find another woman to spend her time with. Or maybe a man…?

"No," She muttered, flashing a smile to the bouncer at the gate surrounding the bar. He smiled back, opening the locked entrance for her. "No men tonight."

"That's a shame, I get off in an hour." The bouncer replied, earning a light laugh from her as she swatted his arm.

"I'd get you off a whole lot faster than that!" Jennifer winked, running a slinky arm over the bouncer's broad arms and shoulders.

Several hours and drinks later, Jennifer found herself stumbling home alone. A college boy named Eric had flirted with her all night, buying drink after drink in a vain attempt to get into her panties. She'd wooed him for a while, rubbing the front of his jeans until he was swollen before going back to her drink. When he finally asked her back to his hotel room, she just shook her head and walked off, leaving him in a bad spot, as he couldn't stand from his stool without everyone seeing how aroused he'd become.

Too bad for him, she thought drunkenly to herself as she sashayed down the sidewalk. Taking a moment to smooth out a wrinkle in her skirt, Jennifer savored the silence of her street.

The sounds of the bands were distant, far off cries

that echoed throughout the town. The French Quarter, alive with the sound of music, rocked and thrummed to the beat. But here on St. Benedict lane the festivities had died down. Walking slowly down the narrow sidewalk, Jennifer fished out her house key as she approached her home; a lean townhouse with shuttered windows and a wide stoop, two statues depicting praying angels flanking the dull red door.

Looking around the street, Jennifer didn't see the clunker of an Oldsmobile that her father drove around town. "Probably out enjoying all the parties..." She murmured as she unlocked the front door. "Damn drunk! Doubt he left anything for me to even eat."

Flipping on the light to the living room, Jennifer kicked off her shoes. Looking around the messy little room, from the flat screen TV on the wall to the leather couch littered with remotes, Jennifer could only breathe deep and struggle to stand straight. Stumbling into the darkened kitchen, Jennifer made her way to the fridge in search of something cold to drink. The hot southern night had left a sheen of sweat on her dusky skin and walking home had sobered her up far too much for her liking. She walked into the kitchen just as the front door clicked closed.

Wincing at the bright light coming from within the fridge, she fished out a bottle of beer from the bottom drawer. She grabbed the bottle opener hanging from the fridge's door handle, quickly popping off the top before swigging down a fourth of the bitter beverage in a single pull, smiling as some of the foam fell to her cleavage.

"Hmm... now I'm thinking about beefcake instead of cheesecake. Maybe I should've taken Eric up on his offer?" Jennifer mused. She walked out of the kitchen, tripping over her shoes, which were uncharacteristically set just outside the kitchen.

"Damn things!" She cursed, kicking them away. Looking up, she nearly choked on her beer when she saw the front door wide open, slightly creaking as it swayed in the wind.

"Didn't I lock the door?" She growled, setting her beer down as she jumped to close it again. "Dad really needs to get off his ass and fix this door already, shouldn't be opening cause of a stiff breeze!"

Picking her beer back up, Jennifer plopped down onto the couch, snatching up a remote. Undoing her belt and laying it over the back of the leather sofa, Jennifer moved into a position in which she could relax. Flipping through the channels with one hand while unzipping the side of her miniskirt with the other, Jennifer shed the confining article of clothing before scratching at her upper thigh.

"To think I could have been fucking that blonde tonight if it weren't for that old pervert..." she groused, taking another sip of her beer as she skipped to the movie channels. "God, I am so horny right now! Damn frat boy was even looking good for a while..."

Finishing off the beer, Jennifer surfed the adult networks, looking for something... exciting to watch. Settling on an adult film about nurses, Jennifer got up to turn on the air conditioner and get another beer.

Returning to the living room, Jennifer spared a moment to crank up the air conditioning, turning the dial all the way to the coldest setting. While this would piss her Dad off when he got home, Jennifer reasoned she paid for her own expenses; she deserved to be comfortable in her own home after a frustrating night. She tripped on the rug, looking down to see some crumbs she hadn't noticed before.

"God," she rolled her eyes. "Dad really needs to stop living like such a pig. I mean, clean up after yourself, why don't you?"

Settling back onto the couch next to the remotes, Jennifer tipped her beer back as she watched the opening credits end and a buxom redhead enter the frame, dressed in a ridiculous parody of a nurse's outfit, complete with a pair of white high heels.

"God, I can't believe guys are into this… though she does have a nice ass." Jennifer mused, allowing her hand to slide down her hips. "Maybe I can get into this…"

The movie played on like a typical porno did, with the redheaded woman checking on a studly patient with too many tattoos, who promptly had the woman by her hair and bent over his lap, lavishing her tongue all over his throbbing manhood. Jennifer could feel the all-too-familiar heat rising, a heat she carefully stoked with her fingers over her skirt.

After thirty minutes, Jennifer had somehow found herself sans her panties, her bare flesh chilly and sticking to the leather of the furniture. Legs splayed apart as wide as she could force them, she panted as she fought to bring about her orgasm. Letting out a throaty moan, Jennifer matched her own questing fingers speed to that of the man eating out the actress on the big screen.

"Yeah, make her scream!" Jennifer slurred. "Yes, that's it right there…"

Jennifer's pleasure was cut short as something crashed in the kitchen, the sound of plates falling over themselves and into the sink ringing off the walls. It must have been her own imagination, but she thought she heard footsteps as well.

"Hello?" She called out, unable to resist fingering herself all the while. "Is anyone there?"

No reply came. Taking another sip of her beer, Jennifer held the cold bottle for a few moments longer than necessary, allowing her hand to grow cold and wet. Her arousal only growing more demanding, she thrust a finger deep into herself, curling it enough to send shivers of pleasure running all over her body.

I should really check and see what that was… but I just can't stop! Jennifer thought through the haze of alcohol and arousal. So close!

Turning back towards the screen, she paused as her eyes settled on the black leather belt and its silver buckle, hanging over the back of the couch; as if possessed, she reached out and grabbed it, her arm moving on its own as she continued to pleasure herself. Mind awash with pleasure, Jennifer rolled her eyes back into her head as she wrapped the belt around her neck, buckling it on the sixth peg, just tight enough to where she had slight trouble breathing.

Moving her hand to her center, Jennifer resumed her thrusting, moaning as she happily regained her passionate peak. Breathing in shallow, ragged breathes she quickly closed in on her own release, a release she'd been trying to achieve all night. She bit her lower lip as she choked back a moan, arching her back as she reached the edge of orgasm.

Only for her hand to slow down, her fingers sluggish. Sputtering indignantly, she could only look on in frustration as her hand ran over her pubic mound, her fingers leisurely circling her clitoris, just as she'd done earlier in the evening.

"What the hell?" Jennifer gasped, looking down at her hand in desperation. But all it did was tease her with tantalizing glides. She heard a devilish giggle to her right, but found she couldn't turn to look.

Her other hand moved up to her throat, where the belt was buckled, pulling on the end to unbuckle it, tightening the belt slowly to the next peg, leaving her gasping for air. Grunting in pain and pleasure, Jennifer whined as her hand began moving of its own accord once more, forcing three fingers into her tight opening. Letting out a choked gasp, Jennifer forced herself to look over at the remotes, and gasped.

Sitting on the leather cushion was a gingersnap cookie in the shape of a man, frosting eyes and mouth twisted into an angry snarl, sitting next to him was a shapely half-baked dough girl with several strands of black hair jutting from the scalp. It didn't have any facial features, but it did have a strand of black thread wrapped around its neck in a parody of what Jennifer was doing. The scowling gingersnap turned back to the feminine one before forcing it to play with itself.

Jennifer wanted to scream as her hand mimicked the movement, but all she could do was groan in pain, her hand tightened the belt another peg, the thick leather pressing deep into her throat. Tears welled at the corners of her eyes. Above her own choking sobs, Jennifer heard the simple clacking of hard soled shoes on linoleum from behind her, along with the chuckles of the strange cookie, playing with its half-baked doughy Barbie doll.

Sadly, her head remained firmly looking forward, her eyes watching the torrid displays of carnal lust before her on the television. Jennifer could hear the deep breathing of someone, a man, as they entered the living room… but something seemed off… there were three distinct steps being taken, not two; almost as if the person possessed an extra leg.

Her eyes went wide: or a cane!

"You told me," Came the rich voice of the old man from earlier in the night, "to go to Hell young lady."

Sauntering around the couch, the old man strode into her line of sight, pulling off his tinted spectacles. In the recessed lighting of the living room, he appeared even older than he had in the alleyway, his face heavy with age. His hands, both covered in black satin gloves, were knotted from arthritis. A single gold ring sat on the middle finger of his left hand, which rested atop the skull on his cane. In the other hand, he held the doughy cookie creature, its legs splayed wide.

The man locked eyes with Jennifer before glancing down at her hand, still furiously masturbating. "I knew from our brief exchange that your passions ran deep, but my oh my, I had no idea they were this serious!"

"H-how...?" Jennifer choked out, her breath coming up short thanks to the belt slowly crushing her throat.

"How did I do this? Or how did I get in here? How what child, you best speak up if you want me to know what you're asking about!" The old man laughed, resting his cane against the wall as he reached into his jacket, pulling a long silver pin between two slender fingers. "Let's see if we can help you out a little, shall we?"

More laughter came from the couch, and Jennifer slowly looked over to see there were now five gingersnaps. The man unceremoniously dropped the half-cooked creation in front of them, handing the silver pin to the original gingersnap man.

The cookie curled over, rubbing the shaft of the pin up and down before looking over his shoulder with a savage grin. The others, obviously amused by the antics of their leader, swatted their knees and each other's backs. The gingersnap brandished the pin, before ramming it into the crotch of the half-baked doll, forcing Jennifer's eyes to roll back in her head as a piercing agony slammed into her loins, stopping her rising climax dead in its tracks, almost pinning it in location where it squirmed and writhed, the pleasure and pain intermingling. Her hand continued to move, but nothing seemed to get her any closer. She glared at the old man.

"Only good girls get their rewards… and telling me to go to Hell? No good girl disrespects her elders." The old man hummed as the gingersnaps gave each other high-fives. "I would say this might teach you a lesson about manners little girl, but that would imply you're going to make it past tonight."

"P-please…" Jennifer gasped both from her lack of air and her fingers sliding back into her aching center once more. What was once sending waves of pleasure was now growing sore, and raw. Her fingers went from gentle caresses to violent strokes, her nails scraping her inner walls and lips harshly.

"Oh, now you have manners! All it took was a little black magic, baking, and a dirty movie and you found yourself a little humility." The old man cackled, reaching once more into his jacket, this time pulling a crushed velvet bag. "You told me to go to Hell little girl; you disrespected me! Now I'm gonna show you what such words will cost you!"

Pulling a pinch of blue powder from the bag, the man leaned over Jennifer's writhing body to smear the strange substance beneath her nose. It smelled faintly of the ocean… as well as something dark and primal. Breathing rapidly to compensate for her strangulation, Jennifer felt light headed, the outer edges of her vision growing dark as her head pounded. The man reached down to the couch, grabbing the television remote before turning off the obscene movie behind him.

With her last breath, just before her eyes closed, Jennifer glimpsed the black screen reflecting the room behind her. The hellish gingersnaps had climbed to the top of the couch and were tightening the belt around her neck, even as she struggled for breath and tore into herself with her dainty fingers, pain roiled over her trapped pleasure.

A sharp shock in her groin as well as warmth spreading over her lower legs had her bring a hand up to her face, her arm moving woodenly. The hand dripped red, with chunks of pink wedged beneath her fingernails. Her last thoughts, a jumble of pointless ideas of how to escape or being rescued, were cut short when the gingersnaps pulled on the belt one last time, causing her to black out.

The darkness consumed her, pulling her into an ever expanding well of icy death.

Is this Hell? Am I in Hell for all the things I've done? She thought bitterly, looking about the void hoping to see something, anything.

But there was nothing.

Wait... off in the distance, there was a light. Turning, she tried to move towards the light, like she had so often heard in movies. This would be how she would move on, possibly to Heaven! She could feel shivers of pleasure wrack her frame, her mouth opening as sweet release edged closer... only for the light to be a single flame in a darkened room of denial.

She blinked her eyes a few times, a dull ache

throbbing in her loins, wrapped around the climax that she'd yet to achieve. Even now, she could feel it lingering, moments away, but she couldn't move! She tried to lift her head but found that she couldn't. Looking around, there was an oil lantern burning bright off the wall she was flush to, atop a sturdy metal counter. The smells of herbs and spices assaulted her senses, with the sounds of clattering pans and high-pitched cackling enunciated by bright flashes of fiery light. Her breathing was shallow, almost to the point where she wasn't getting enough air.

"Ah," the old man said, coming into view. "I see you're awake!"

She glared at him but found herself unable to talk. He must have read her mind because he ran a gloved hand through his hair before talking.

"A simple cocktail of puffer fish extract and ground rattlesnake skin was enough to start the process," the old man smiled. "I'm, from what I've been told, a strange man with unique tastes. For example, I'm a Bokor and a cook. I have the best restaurant in the city thanks to a pinch of black magic and the manpower of my zombie workers."

Jennifer growled low in her throat but said nothing. It was difficult getting enough breath to keep the stars out of her vision, ignoring her desires was almost blindingly impossible.

"Now as I'm sure you've noticed, you're somewhere you've never been. I'd give you the grand tour, but I feel that to be unnecessary. We've a restaurant to run and I can't waste time explaining the ropes to the new girl."

Leaning over her body, the man took a long and heavy sniff of her skin, causing Jennifer to shiver from the profane movement.

"As delicious as you smell I think you should get dressed! You have your first shift coming up, and we have discerning guests to tend to." The bokor said. He clapped his hands, and her numbed body sat up, causing her vision to swim. She felt a pressure next to her, pushing into her side, and she looked down to see what it was.

A folded uniform had been her pillow and, try and resist as much as she could, she pulled on the clothes. The outfit showed off her legs with black silken stockings, and a plaited mini skirt that stopped just below her ass. Her button-up top was tight around her neck, and she had a collar she put on over the indentions left by her belt. She desperately wanted to rub her fingers over her aching vulva, but her body refused to do anything she told it to do, instead, dressing as slowly as it could.

Looking around as the gingersnap men tied her shoelaces, she stared in awe at the gigantic kitchen, manned by numerous stiff-moving figures. There was a tall chef searing meat on a grill while a baker, aided by a dozen gingersnaps, stirred at some cheddar dough. Looking to her left, she saw a mirror and jerked back.

Her mouth was sewn shut, her eyes surrounded by black eyeshadow to show off the luminescent orbs. Her skin looked taut over her bones. The gingersnaps scampered off as the old man walked up to her, offering his arm to her. She took it with dead hands, glaring at him as he walked her towards some stairs. "I see you noticed the addition! Those stitches will keep your mouth good and silent, at least until you earn the right to speak again."

She tried to say something, but only nodded slowly. He had complete control over her, and she knew it.

"All of our waitresses are kept in the room next to the stairs," he said, motioning with his hand. The door to the room was metallic, and it looked like a morgue, several nude women laying out on metal tables, their eyes wide open and their mouths stitched closed. The old man turned her attention upstairs. "Now, here are the rules. You try to fight me, you get to be an ingredient for a nice meat dish. You obey and work hard, you get to become a chef. The chefs have a little freedom, like the ability to talk... the ability to find relief, so to speak."

Jennifer growled, but couldn't voice anything beyond a low grumble. The old man chuckled and adjusted his glasses. "One last stop before you take a tray up to room fourteen."

They passed the stairs and through an open doorway, the word 'Pantry' chiseled above the door.

Looking around, she saw huge sacks of flour and sugar sitting on rough timber shelving, low light coming from another oil lantern. At the back was a young woman, tied up and set atop a barrel, naked with numerous wounds. Upon closer inspection, Jennifer realized it was the girl she'd 'been with' earlier in the night. The thought brought the memory of her juices to Jennifer's lips.

Her loins flared within her, making her stomach

turn as the fire within raged. It pleaded with her through its ache to find something to stimulate her to the finish line. She'd fuck anybody right now if she could just make a damn move on her own!

"Your little girlfriend was most uncooperative. I just wanted to show you how we deal with ingredients here..." The bokor smiled.

Frozen, she watched as several gingersnaps ran from behind them, one dragging a three-inch paring knife as it approached. The cookies climbed the barrel and poked her in sensitive spots with their pointed edges. The one with the knife climbed up slowly while two who'd already scaled to the top pulled a cork from the barrel. Jennifer could hardly see due to the poor lighting, shadows danced across every inch of the room in a crude mockery of life. She smelled a heady scent, like that of pennies mixed with a woman's arousal... it would have normally been alluring to Jennifer.

Now it just sickened her.

She watched and shook her head minutely as the gingersnap with the paring knife stabbed it into the woman's inner thigh, carving off several small flaps of meat. The girl screamed and thrashed, but her restraints were too tight. She didn't seem to bleed too much, what little blood that dribbled oozing into the barrel.

Once the sadistic gingersnaps had what they wanted, they ran back into the kitchen between her and the old man's legs.

"Hmmm... the leg of lamb is popular tonight I see." The old man noted before guiding Jennifer over to a waiting area, where a large brown tray sat, a steaming plate of rice and beans with some spicy pulled meat staring up at her next to a glass of blood red wine. "Looks like a regular is here. Be sure to treat him well…"

And with that, the old man walked off. Jennifer found herself compelled to carry the tray upstairs and into the halls of a cozy mansion. The main hall was lined with numbered rooms, the entryway guarded by two large men with mouths stitched shut, just like hers. They looked older than most of the other bokor controlled men and women, making her wonder what would end up happening to her.

She found room fourteen and knocked three times. How she knew to do that, she didn't know, but a response from the other side prompted her to open the door.

The room was comfortable, with a small television playing a football game while an older black man sat at a circular red table, rubbing his hands together. Jennifer nearly dropped the tray when she recognized her father, gut and glasses and all.

"My oh my, they sent up a cutie tonight! You can't tell me your name I know, but I need to talk to the management and see if I can… rent you for an evening. You look just like me slut of a daughter… it would make it all the more delicious seeing as that slut runs around fucking everyone, teasing me just like her mother used to. I get you for a night, I'll pound you till my balls are empty!"

Jennifer would've gagged at his comments, but her body just moved to set up the plate and drink, her numb flesh feeling the pressure of her father's hand running up her ass as she leaned over. She could feel the pleasure within her rolling about, begging for the attention. She almost gagged when she turned and let him peer down her cleavage, the way his eyes widened both humiliating and intoxicating to her pent up frustrations.

"The other girls have all been wild in the sack, quiet because of the stitches, but absolutely relentless once you got their skirts bunched up! And the fact you look like my daughter, why... I got to taste you next!"

This is Hell... Jennifer thought, whimpering. She felt her father's hand cup her ass, her body leaning into him with a purr as arousal dripped from her moistened panties. When he slapped her ass as she walked out, she almost broke the control and turned to mount him, heedless of what the ramifications would be. But the control the bokor had over her was absolute. She closed the door, shedding quiet tears of frustration as another throb from her core roared at the familiar scent she'd smelled in the pantry; the smell of pennies and arousal, coming from her father's drink.

-END

To learn more about the author, Nicholas Paschall, find his author bio at http://www.grivantepress.com/

Dear Reader,

Thank you for joining us on this crazy adventure that was MASHED. We hope you enjoyed reading the stories as much as we enjoyed creating them. The seventeen authors in this book are all Indie Authors and your support is greatly appreciated.

If you enjoyed MASHED, please consider taking a moment and leaving a review on Amazon, Goodreads, Facebook or wherever you as a reader hang out online. A review doesn't have to be complicated or lengthy. It can be as simple as, I liked it because… and then list a couple of things you enjoyed about the story. That's all!

Thank you for your time and support!

-Grivante & The Mashed Author Team

P.S. Want to see another volume of MASHED? Send us a note at mashed@grivantepress.com and let us know you'd love to see more MASHED stories!

Now, turn the page to enjoy a special preview of another Grivante Press publication!

"I'm sorry sir, it doesn't appear to be a rodent problem."

"What do you mean? Not rodents? All that scratching and scurrying all night long? What type of bugs can be making that kind of racket?"

The man from the pest control company looked down and rubbed his name tag, which read 'Burt', with his right hand. "Sir, do you know if this area may have once been home to a graveyard?"

Mr. Pembleton's brow furrowed. What kind of question was that? "Well, yeah, this whole area was once Pakatini tribal lands. My neighbor Shirley told me there are small family buried plots all over. Just last week, the Hembrooks over on Lancaster, dug up a pile of bones and some kind of am-let thingy. They threw it all out in the trash. Bones in their back yard. Can you believe it?"

Mr. Pembleton stopped there, a sparkle of realization dawning. "Wait, are you trying to tell me there are bones down there and a dog or some feral cat got in 'em?"

Burt's eyes widened at that. "Um, no Sir. From the way the earth is disturbed and the scratch marks on the floor joists and foundation, I would say you have a zombie infestation."

Mr. Pembleton blinked twice. He rubbed his grey and black whiskered jaw and adjusted his false teeth, then asked, "How much is that gonna cost?"

"I don't know Sir, we don't handle zombies. We only make living things dead, not, um, dead things dead."

"Who does then?"

Burt, sweating a little from his brow, broke his stance and started checking his pockets. "We, uh, technically aren't supposed to recommend anyone, but, um, there are these brothers. They have a little side business and I've got their card here somewhere. With the apocalypse coming there's been more and more of a need for their services." He was now flipping through his wallet, his pockets having revealed nothing but lint and old cough drop wrappers. He ate them constantly to keep the smell of the poisons he used from making his nose itch.

"Which apocalypse is that? Was it that Nostradumbass fella again? He predicted Hitler and the Obamanation of our country, or wait, I saw one on TV the other day that said George Clooney was the anti-Christ and if he sees his reflection in the mirror at the Vatican—"

"Ah," Burt pulled a tattered business card from his wallet and thrust it at Mr. Pembleton, interrupting his rant. "Here you go!"

Zee Brothers : Zombie Exterminators
Jonah & Judas : Owner Operators
888·867·5309
Ask for Jenny
"We keep the dead, dead!"

Burt made his way to the door.

Mr. Pembleton looked up from the card. "Are these guys any good?"

Burt's hand was on the front door knob. "Well, I don't know, Sir. No one I've given their card to has ever called to tell me, I just know they're a bit... different." He twisted the knob and swung the door open.

Mr. Pembleton opened his mouth to speak but Burt spoke first.

"Best of luck Mr. P., no charge for the inspection. Have a Pest Free Day!"

Slam!

Burt scurried down the drive, popping a cough drop into his mouth and breathing in the sweet menthol, never hearing, but knowing exactly what Mr. Pembleton had wanted to ask: "What do you mean, different?"

Inside, Mr. Pembleton's eyes drifted back to the card. He shambled off to find his phone, muttering under his breath. "Different, huh? This better not cost too much."

Ring!

"Zee Brothers!" a male voice answered. "How can we help you?"

"Uh, yes, is Jenny available?"

Laughter erupted from the other end so loud that even though Mr. Pembleton's hearing wasn't the best, he had to hold the phone away from his ear until it died down.

"This is Judas, Owner, How—, OW!"

There was a clambering and clamoring on the other end for a moment, then a different voice came back on the phone. "This is Jonah, Owner of Zee Brothers, Zombie Exterminators. How can I help you?"

"My name is Larry Pembleton. I live at 547 Westerly Drive, the pest control man just left and he gave me your card. He thinks I might have a zombie infestation."

"Mhm," the voice on the other end responded. "Just a minute, Mr. Pembleton."

For a moment all Mr. Pembleton could hear were muffled voices as it sounded like someone had placed their hand over the receiver.

"Sir," the second voice came back on the line, "Ok, what else can you tell me?"

"Well, Burt asked if the house was built over any kind of cemetery."

"And is it?"

"Well, yes, yes, it is. Most of this development was built over the old Pakatini Reservation for the new county dump and our fabulous gated community of Winter Oaks. Progress, you know. The Pakatinis all died off years ago."

"And you said Burt? From Pests B' Gone?"

"Yeah, that's what his tag said." Mr. Pembleton was getting annoyed. "Look mister, how much is this going to cost?"

"Mr. Pembleton, I need you to listen really closely to me. The infestation, is it in the crawl space under your house?"

"Why, does that cost extra?"

"No. Look, it's almost sundown. I need you to go and make sure that Burt closed and locked the cover to your crawl space."

"Alright, alright," Mr. Pembleton grumbled as he got up out of his chair. "But seriously, how much is this going to cost me?" He shuffled off down the hall to the closet.

Behind the closed door, the hatch to the crawlspace was indeed open. A skeletal hand of bone and decayed flesh fumbled around, looking for leverage to lift itself.

"We'll talk price in a minute Mr. Pembleton. Let's just make sure that thing is locked up tight for now. These native zombie types generally only rise after sundown and they're usually searching for, or upset about, something. Can you tell me if you've been doing any yard work lately and maybe disturbed some bones?"

Mr. Pembleton came to a stop just outside the closet door. "Now listen here, mister. I don't know what kind of negotiation tactics you're playing at, but all these games ain't gonna make me do anything more till you give me a price! And I ain't done no landscaping, it was the Hembrooks over on Lancaster. If they were the ones that caused this, then they the ones that need to be paying for it! I don't care if he's president of the Homeowners'

Association and what not!!" Mr Pembleton was full on shouting now, his hand resting on the knob and he pulled the door open.

"I keep my grass cut, just like it says in our covenants and if he up and disturbed some kind of zombie omelet he's gonna pay!"

"Zombie omelet?" Jonah asked.

"Ahhhhh!"

Mr. Pembleton fell over backwards, more in fright then from the weight of the small frame lunging at him. The phone fell from his grasp and his screams were soon replaced by the rending of flesh and gurgling of blood.

Then a low guttural moan, "Ommmmllet."

His brother raised his eyebrows as he watched him. "Well? We got a customer or not?"

Jonah sighed, his lips flapping as he did so. "No, I'm pretty sure he just died."

"What!? I knew you shoulda let me talk to him!" Judas's head bounced with each word, spit flying.

Jonah glared at his brother. "Burt left the crawl space open when he left."

"Burt from Pests B' Gone?"

"Yeah. That Burt."

"Well, shit. What we gonna do now, Jonah?"

Jonah shook his head, "Load up Sasha. We're gonna have to go clean this up before it gets outta hand."

Judas stood, grabbing a shotgun from the couch next to him. "Wait a minute. What was that about a zombie omelet? Did that guy have some sort of weird cannibal fetish?"

Jonah shrugged. "I've no idea, but don't forget to feed Fido before we go."

Sasha, the brothers' 1950s Chevy pick-up truck, tooled down the road, a small stream of smoke puffing from Jonah's open window as he dragged and released on his pipe. On the other side of the bench seat, past the giant 8-ball gear shifter, Judas sat with his own window down, lip bulging and his door covered in dark gooey strands of tobacco spit. The engine rumbled like gentle thunder behind the sounds of Jonah's classical music CD.

Spit! "Really, Jonah, didn't we listen to this last time?"

Jonah puffed away on his pipe that he held in his three fingered left hand, the gear shift in his right and his knee guiding the wheel. He said nothing.

Judas slipped his hand along the dash toward the eject button. Before he could depress it, Jonah's hand flew off the vibrating shifter and smashed his brother's hand against the dash. "Driver's choice!"

"Ow!" Judas let out a scream as his brother pressed harder into his hand, illustrating the point. "But you always drive!" Brown spittle oozed into the whiskers on his chin.

"You haven't passed your driving test."

"Well that thing ain't fair. It's got all them choices to make and signs to memorize."

Jonah raised his left hand, the pipe pinched between

his thumb and pointer finger, wiggling his middle finger and the two tiny stumps where his index and pinky used to be. "Life ain't fair, Judas."

Judas pulled his hand away and sulked. They drove in silence for a few minutes. "Are we there yet?" Judas asked.

"No. We had to go around, there was some sort of taco truck accident on the highway between Winter Oaks and the new dump, grease all over the road."

"Where did you hear that?"

"It was on the news before we left."

"Hmph." Judas slunk down in his seat, rubbing the palm of his left hand. "That hurt, Jonah."

Jonah turned and glared at his younger brother. "Well, so did this!" He waved the two stumps on his left hand at Judas and then shoved his pipe halfway into his mouth but, feeling stubborn, he left it there as they turned onto the road leading up to Winter Oaks.

They pulled to a stop just before the large metal gate which closed off the elitist community of Winter Oaks from the rest of the world. The gate was black iron with large spikes at the top and a stand of metal trees that met at the middle above the words, 'Winter Oaks'.

Aside from a number of small pedestrian entry gates that dotted the brick and mortar barrier around the community, this was the only real entrance.

"How we gonna get in there, Jonah?"

Jonah looked down at the little keypad outside his

window, set his pipe on the seat next to him and reached over and typed in the numbers 0420. Nothing happened.

"Hmm." He sat, thought for a moment and then typed in four more numbers. Still nothing.

"Jonah?"

"Yeah?"

"Did you try 0420?"

"Yes."

"Didn't work?"

Jonah turned to look at Judas. He looked at the closed gate, then back at his brother and raised his eyebrows.

"Oh. Right." Judas turned his head and looked out the window, slipping a finger in his lip and clearing out the black chunks of chew and tossing them on the pavement. His lip continued to stick out even when empty.

Jonah kept punching four digit combinations into the box to no avail.

"Jonah?"

"Yes, Judas, I tried our birth year too."

"No, Jonah, look over there." Judas pointed out the window and through the gate to a yard a couple of blocks up the road.

Jonah leaned forward, his left arm still dangling out the window. There was a shadowy shape moving slowly across the yard of a cookie cutter ranch house. "Shit."

"We gotta get in there Jonah, they could be everywhere." He slipped a new fat wad of chewing tobacco into his lip and lifted the shotgun off his lap.

Jonah turned back to the box and screamed as a cold hand wrapped around his dangling arm. The woman standing there let go and jumped away, tripping over the leash of the small dog at her feet. She stumbled backward until her startled momentum carried her ass over tea kettle onto a small grassy knoll, next to the brick wall.

"Oh shit, oh shit!" Judas, having only heard his brother scream and then seen the flailing body fall away, scrambled. Swinging the shotgun up, he smacked himself in the face with the barrel, knocking the fresh wad of chewing tobacco free and down his throat.

Jonah jettisoned himself from the truck and rushed to offer the woman a hand. "Are you alright, miss?"

The woman's shiny strawberry-blonde hair covered her face, she blew it up and out of the way as she leaned forward and giggled.

Jonah's mouth fell open and his heart pounded. He self-consciously stuck his three fingered left hand into the back pocket of his jeans.

Judas, meanwhile, coughing and spitting tobacco from his mouth, got out of the truck, shotgun in hand and made his way around the back. He too stopped short, heart pounding, when he saw the beautiful woman lying on the ground. "Sasha!" He shouted, then his face turned green and he doubled over to his knees. "Ughhh."

The woman looked at the enamored faces of the brothers as her giggling died down and she was over-run by her dog's yelping bark. "Shh pup," she said, then her face wrinkled as Judas began to vomit. "Oh my."

Jonah stretched out his right arm, offering his good hand. "May I help you up? Please."

She glanced at his hand and took it, then turned back to look at Judas. "Why did he call me Sasha and then throw up all over the place?"

Jonah pulled her up from the ground. As she came to her feet, she stumbled, a little lightheaded and he pulled his other hand free to steady her. She saw his hand and grabbed it with her own hand, examining the missing fingers.

"Oh no, what happened?"

He pulled his hand away, but her grip held firm and he ended up pulling her into an almost full embrace against his chest. "It was an on-the-job accident," he said, standing tall and trying to regain his composure.

He stepped out of the embrace and answered her other questions. "He called you Sasha, because you look exactly like the Russian supermodel, Sasha Borinvisky. We have her calendar on the wall of our garage. I have no idea why that made him throw up." He turned away from her and stepped toward his younger brother.

"Judas, what's the matter?"

Judas looked up at the two of them. Long gooey strands littered with black chunks of tobacco hung from his open mouth. He repositioned himself, putting the shotgun across his knees and groaned.

"Um," JJ said, looking a little worried, "Do you guys have plans to abduct Sasha the Supermodel? What's with the shotgun?"

Judas spat. "We're exterminators."

She laughed. "What do you exterminate with a shotgun?"

"What can't we?" answered Judas.

"It just doesn't seem like it would be very effective against ants or even cockroaches, though I've seen some big enough to warrant the heavy artillery."

"We don't do bugs ma'am," Jonah answered. "We deal with larger problems." He handed her a card.

"No shit? Zombie Exterminators?"

Judas had some stability in his stomach and stood taller, nodding. "Yes, that's us. We're the Zee Brothers. Judas and Jonah."

"And wait, that's why you have a shotgun? You thought I was a zombie?"

Judas stumbled over his words. "Well, no, er, yes. Jonah started screaming and I couldn't see what was going on, then I swallowed my chew trying to get out of the truck."

The woman laughed, jutting her chin forward. Her hair fell off her shoulder and down over her face, she flung her head the other way and sent it back in an arc. The street light caught her face and set it aglow.

The brothers both wore identical expressions, mouths open slightly, Judas's with bits of black in his teeth, their eyes transfixed on opposite corners of her smile. She looked from one face to the next and her own smile widened, followed by both of theirs until the three of them had wide toothy grins.

Their trio of reverie was interrupted by the persistent yelping of her dog. She broke their gaze and bent down to pet him. "Quiet boy." The muscles in her slender legs flexed and both brothers admired her tight shorts and the roundness of her behind.

The brother's eyes drifted up to one another, Judas pointed at her and mouthed "Dibs."

Jonah shook his head, "No way!" he mouthed back.

Judas opened his mouth to say more, but stopped as she stood back up, her dog now calmed.

"So what are you two doing here?" she asked.

"We have a client," Jonah said, "A Mr. Pembleton."

"Don't know him," she said, "but I'm only here visiting my aunt and uncle for the week. Does he, um, have zombies?"

Judas jumped into the conversation, "An omelet full of them."

The woman tilted her head and looked at Judas. "He has a zombie omelet?"

"No," Jonah said.

"It's what you said he said."

Jonah glared at his brother.

"I said, I didn't know what he said, it sounded like omelet."

"Why would he say he had a zombie omelet if he didn't have none, Jonah?"

"I don't know Judas." He looked at the woman shrugging, "We got disconnected before we could get more details."

"Oh no," the woman said. "Do you think he's been eaten?"

"I don't know, we were trying to figure out how to get in there," he nodded toward the gate, "so we could check."

"Oh! Let me put the code in for you." She ran over to the box and pushed buttons until there was a click and a whir and the gate parted in the middle.

"Thank you," the brothers said in unison.

"No problem. Just get in there and make sure he's alright. Better hurry though, the gate doesn't wait long."

Jonah started toward the truck, when Judas spoke up, causing him to cringe and stop.

"Miss?"

"Yes, cutie?" She smiled at him.

"He-he," Judas laughed and looked down, kicking his boots together. "Um, be careful in there, if he does have zombies, others may too. We thought we saw one walking in that yard over there."

They all turned and looked, but no one was there now.

"Don't worry about me," she said reaching up and pulling down the zipper of her leather jacket. It opened, revealing a tight black tank top with a pair of pointy nipples sticking through it. Both brothers' mouths fell open. She opened the left side of her coat further, revealing the butt of a pink revolver. "I've got The Pink Lady."

With a clack the gate began to rumble back the way it had come, startling them back to reality.

"Shit, c'mon Judas, get in the truck!" Jonah opened his door and hopped in, then leaned out the window. "Sorry about knocking you over and thanks for all your help." Next to him Judas slammed his door shut and Jonah grabbed the big 8-ball shifter and rammed it into first gear.

"Get her name, Jonah!"

"What? Oh, yeah." Jonah leaned his head back out as they began to rumble forward, "What's your name, miss?"

"You boys can call me JJ and my dog is Xanadu!"

…To be continued!

Want to read more of The Zee Brothers?
Check them out at
www.thezeebrothers.com
Or directly on Amazon at
https://www.amazon.com/dp/B013M5DXGC/

Join our newsletter and stay connected!
http://zx.grivantepress.com/MASHEDSIGNUP

GRIVANTE PRESS

Want to have some fun and win some cool prizes?

We want you to prank call The Zee Brothers!

Who are The Zee Brothers?

Jonah & Judas are two brothers in the Zombie Extermination business. Just like any other exterminators, they get phone calls from prospective clients and go out and do inspections to determine what needs to be done.

Unfortunately, due to the nature of the pests, this usually turns into a bloody mess in a hurry. Most often, where Jonah & Judas are concerned, it's generally pretty funny as well.

While the brothers are serious about what they do, there is one night a year where they will not answer their phone.

You see, Jonah & Judas get a lot of prank calls to their Zombie Exterminators phone #, but it's the worst on Halloween night.

That's the one night a year when people think it's funniest to harass them. They don't answer the phone and they don't go out. All those costumes and people in zombie make-up are a recipe for disaster for guys ready to shoot anything that's dead but still moving, so they just stay home and let the phone ring.

The messages range from people making fun of zombie extermination, people pretending they are being attacked, to people saying zombies aren't real. The list goes on and on. The next morning they nurse their hangovers and listen to the Halloween madness.

That's where you come in!

We want you to call and leave your craziest, zaniest message about zombies or zombie exterminators to Jonah & Judas. Pretend you're a potential client or just be a funny prankster.

What's in it for you?
Your call could be featured in The Zee Brothers Vol.3 both as text in the book and possibly even the audio from your call in the audiobook. We'll also broadcast some of our favorites across our social media, bringing you untold

fame... no fortune, but we promise as much fame as your humor creates.

PRIZES!

The top 3 prank callers will all win signed copies of The Zee Brothers Books 1-3! And the contents of your call will likely be featured in book 3.

Other prizes may include posters, prints, bookmarks, apparel and more.

(Grand Prizes will be sent out after the release of book 3 mid-2018) Random prizes will be given out all year long.

How do you participate?

Call the Grivante Press offices at 208-352-2102 and at the beep, pretend you are leaving a message for Jonah & Judas. You are more likely to win if you make us laugh, good luck!

Contest Rules:

Must be 18 Years Old at the time of the phone call.

After you've left your message, make sure and pause a moment and then give your call back number, name and an email address so that we can get in touch with you if you win.

CONTEST ENTRY PERIOD ENDS 1/1/18

Winners will be chosen by 1/31/18.

Need something to listen to while you read?
Enjoy the Dark Gothic Rock of Frostbite!
Available at
http://www.frostbiteofficial.com/purchase

CPSIA information can be obtained
at www.ICGtesting.com
Printed in the USA
FFOW03n0539200417
34749FF